HER DRA
PROTEC꜑ ᴏʀ

BLACK CLAW DRAGONS: BOOK 2

Roxie Ray

© 2020

Disclaimer

This is a work of fiction. Names, places, characters and events are all fictitious for the reader's pleasure. Any similarities to real people, places, events, living or dead are all coincidental.

Contents

Prologue

Charlotte

The steak sizzled in the cast iron pan as I danced around the kitchen. Logan was due home at any moment, and he'd totally forgotten it was our six-month anniversary. Six months might not have sounded like much to some people, but I had a history of short, volatile relationships. I was proud to hit six months.

Steak, potatoes, broccoli and cheese. His favorites. It was almost done, and he'd be walking in the door any moment.

The day had passed quickly. I got up early and cleaned our apartment from top to bottom before shopping for the ingredients for dinner. We'd only lived together for about a month, but I had three days off, so I put in a little extra effort to clean up. We'd settle into a routine eventually.

My phone blared out the nineties pop I loved to dance to as I cleaned and cooked. As I wiped the kitchen table down, I shook my booty. When Logan got here, we'd eat, then have dessert. Or maybe dessert first. On the table, if I was lucky.

Logan and I were incredibly passionate in all areas. We argued a lot, but we made up a lot, too. We were both so opinionated that sometimes we butted heads, but that worked for us. I'd finally found a man who could keep up with me.

Humming, I put out the plates, flipped the steaks, and peeked at the potatoes in the oven. I cheated with the broccoli, steaming it in the microwave and using jarred cheese sauce.

Who cared? It was yummy.

The sound of the front door slamming goosed me. I lit the candles and took off the ratty old apron I'd thrown on to keep my dress clean.

"Welcome home." I cheered when Logan walked into the kitchen.

It didn't take me long to figure out something was wrong.

"What the fuck is all this?" His suit was half untucked and his normally impeccable hair was all mussed.

"I made dinner," I said with my eyebrows up. "Are you okay?"

Logan slammed his hand on the table. "No!" When he yelled, his breath whooshed across the table at me, smacking me in the face like a shot of vodka. He'd been drinking.

Shit. He'd told me up front he rarely drank because he was an angry drunk. I didn't mind. I liked the occasional glass—or bottle—of wine, but for the right man I could give up most things.

"We've been together six months today." I kept my voice bright. "I got good steaks, which should be done now."

I didn't want to do anything to trigger more anger. Something had to have happened at work to create such a response in him. "Do you want chives on your potato? I can chop some real quick."

"What the fuck did you do today?" It wasn't a question; it was an accusation.

I put the steaks on a plate to rest and turned the eye off. "Why?"

Logan's face darkened. "Because I want to know. Fucking tell me."

"Okay, I cleaned, got food, and came home and cooked." I grabbed the potholder to get the potatoes out. "Oh, and took a long bath to pamper myself so I'd be beautiful for *you*."

I didn't want to make him angrier on top of whatever had gotten him so riled up, but shit, I worked hard on my day off for this, and he came in like a thundercloud.

"Did you run into Seth?" He jerked out a kitchen chair and sat down.

"Your boss? Yeah, I did. I'd forgotten." He'd been at the grocery store at the same time I was. "He said hello, I said hello. Why?"

"Were you dressed like this?" He waved at my dress, which was snug and black and showed my curves in all the right places.

Looking down at myself, I shook my head, confused why that mattered. He was crossing a line, asking how I dressed at the grocery store, and my wariness about not pissing him off was turning into anger. "No. I wore jeans and a t-shirt. What does that have to do with anything?"

He stood out of the kitchen chair so fast it made me jump. "Why are you such a slut?"

My eyebrows were in danger of flying off the top of my head. I put my hands on my hips and glared at him. "Excuse the fuck outta me?"

"I told you I liked my woman to dress modestly!" he roared.

I was perfectly capable of yelling, too. "And I do dress modestly, but I do that for me, not because you asked me to. I like to look classy."

"You lying bitch." A little piece of spittle flew from his mouth.

He didn't cross the line. He lit it on fire and stomped on it. "He came back to work and told me how hot you looked. You were flaunting it for him, weren't you? Hoping to get a leg up? Fuck the boss, maybe you could get with him instead?"

"You've lost your fucking mind. I can't help it if someone thinks I'm hot." I turned off the oven and threw my potholder down. "I hope you choke on dinner." I turned to walk out of the room. Time to lock myself in the bathroom and read until he calmed down.

He'd never gone this far before, gotten this angry. I didn't know how to deal with it.

When I tried to stalk past him, he grabbed my arm, jerking me around to his front. My hip banged into the table painfully, rattling the dishes. "Hey!" I jerked my arm out of his grip, but he wasn't ready to let go. He grabbed the front of my dress and yanked, throwing me off balance again and ripping my dress down the front, exposing my lacy bra. I lost my balance in my stupid heels and fell against the table again, this time knocking over an empty water glass.

It hit the table and cracked, half of it breaking away.

Logan grabbed my arms in a vice grip and dragged me upright again. My blood pounded in my temple as he spoke, narrowing my vision. "You have to learn you can't embarrass me. I won't be made a fool of." He shook me once, hard.

"Let go of me," I screamed. My head flopped as he shook me again, but I couldn't get my arms free. The moment I realized I couldn't get free, I began to panic.

Twisting my body, I tried to bump him back with my hips. He was too strong and too angry. "Slut!" He pulled me around to face him again and shook me harder until my teeth clacked together with a sharp pain in my jaw.

If I didn't do something, he'd genuinely hurt me. I kicked at his shin with my heel and missed but tried again and made contact. He shoved me backward into the refrigerator with a guttural yell, then continued calling me horrible names as he advanced on me. Every name was like a physical blow to my confidence. Not because I believed him, but it showed me how angry he was and made me fear I wouldn't be able to get away from him. I got to my feet and prepared to try to get around him, my gaze darting around the room to find an escape. I brushed off the filthy names like a splash of water. I'd remember them, but they didn't harm me, not really. Not like he was capable of doing.

Unsure how I'd gotten on the floor, I moaned as I took in my surroundings. The last thing I remembered was worrying about getting around him. Consciousness returned slowly and painfully. My cheek throbbed the most, at least until I moved my head. When I tried to sit up, the back of my head pounded enough to make me dizzy and nauseated. Reaching up, I touched my fingers to the spot that hurt the most. And when I pulled my fingers away, they came back covered in blood.

I hadn't even seen his fist coming. I didn't feel my body hit the floor. I didn't feel my head hit the corner of the small deep freeze beside the refrigerator. Based on my grogginess and the pain in my head, it had happened, knocking me out cold.

Rough, cold cotton pressed against my aching cheek, making me gasp. My eyes flew open to find Logan sitting beside me on the kitchen floor. He'd made a cold compress and held it against the side of my face. Without sitting up, I took it from him so I could press it against my skin with far less force.

"Why did you have to do that?" he asked in a low voice. "This all could've been avoided if you'd behaved in a respectful manner."

I couldn't argue with him. If I did, he'd get angry again. I whimpered as my jaw opened. I didn't think it was broken, but it was sore as hell. "I'm sorry," I whispered.

I wasn't sorry. The first chance I got, I'd be the fuck out of there. But for now, he had to think I was obedient and contrite.

I'd seen that movie. Bitches that stuck around ended up dead. I was not going to be a statistic.

"You'll learn." He pressed a kiss to my hand as I pressed the ice pack on my cheek. It took everything I had not to scream at him not to touch me. "Come on."

After hopping to his feet, he bent over and picked me up off the floor with barely a grunt. That's how much stronger than me he was.

His hands on my ribs sent a shot of pain, but what made me cry out was moving my head. There was no way I didn't have a concussion.

The whole way up the stairs, he crooned in my ear, told me he loved me and promised to take care of me.

I didn't want him to take care of me. I wanted him to fucking leave so I could escape and never see this psycho again.

To my intense dismay, Logan took the next day off work to take care of me. Then I had to wait through the weekend. I definitely should've gone to the hospital, and even suggested it at one point, but he insisted I'd be fine with a bit more rest. Thankfully, I'd been a nurse long enough to know that I was hurt, but not seriously injured. A few days of rest and anti-inflammatories would set me right.

Still, becoming a statistic wasn't in my future. I'd fucked around and let him fool me into thinking he was just passionate. High-spirited. Not fucking psycho.

I hoped I was right about my injuries, because he didn't leave me alone long enough to get the fuck out of the house. The weekend passed in a blur of sleep and pills that Logan got from fuck knows where. At least I recognized them and could tell they were safe. Thank heaven for my training.

Sunday, I realized I had to act more normal or he might try to stay home on Monday, too. I didn't want to get up too early, though, and have to spend the entire day faking complacency and affection. After Logan brought my lunch and I heard the sound of his favorite PlayStation game turn on, I took a long shower.

Damn, I moved like a slug. The headache had faded to a dull throb, but my body was in slow mode. By the time I got out of the shower and dressed, Logan was on his way up to check on me.

"Hey, sunshine. I thought I heard the shower. You need help?"

I turned away from my vanity mirror with a smile plastered on my face and my light blonde hair in a messy bun. "I'm moving slow, but I'm okay. I wanted to get up and move and see if I'll be able to work tomorrow."

He arched an eyebrow. "With your face like that?"

I shrugged. No big deal. "I'll tell them we were in a wreck."

"They'll wonder why you didn't come to your own hospital for treatment."

Blinking, I thought fast. "We went away for the weekend, got in a wreck in a cab, my face hit the headrest in front of me."

He nodded. "If you don't act all slutty again, what we went through…" He said it like I'd been a willing participant in the abuse, "…will never happen again. We care about each other so much. There won't be a reason for me to get that angry again, will there?"

I stepped into his arms and wrapped my hands around his waist. The words that came out of my mouth made me nauseated, but I was nobody's fool. I played the game until I could get away. "Of course not. I didn't do it intentionally, of course. I'd never flirt with another man. But from now on I'll make sure I don't inadvertently come across flirty."

Logan's delighted smile was almost more than I could take. I buried my face in his chest instead of keeping the fake happiness on my face.

"We'll speak no more of it," he crooned in my ear. "It's over. Behind us." His finger touched my jaw with a soft touch, applying a bit of pressure so I'd look up.

With a deep breath, I looked into his eyes vulnerably. "Maybe by tomorrow after work, I'll feel like making up all the way." Fluttering my eyelashes, I prayed he got the hint and wouldn't ask me to sleep with him tonight. "My head still hurts enough to make me want to mostly rest today." It was such a fine line between too sick to fuck and well enough that he didn't have to stay home from work tomorrow.

His eyes lit up. "That will be nice. We can redo our dinner."

I squeezed him around the waist, then released him. "I'm going to take a little nap, okay? I'll come down and cook a simple dinner soon."

He pressed a kiss to my forehead, the only place he hadn't bruised on my head, then turned away. "Enjoy your nap."

Fuck. I'd intended to go down and spend more of the day around him showing him I was okay, but now I was nervous he'd ask for sex. I couldn't give him that, not ever again.

After making a quick pot of spaghetti, I begged off again and went to bed, actually falling asleep. I stirred a teeny bit when Logan came to bed but was actually sore and sleepy enough that I slept through his settling down.

The next morning, I got up when our alarm went off and we started our normal morning routine, which was too busy to say much to each other. Logan was in a cheery mood, whistling as he shaved, and generally making me want to shoot him.

Finally, *finally,* I pressed a kiss to his cheek as he ran out the door with his briefcase. "See you tonight," I called. "Can't wait."

His SUV pulled away from the curb. I let the curtain I'd been peeking behind fall into place once he turned onto the next street and I couldn't see him anymore.

I had a few hours. Very rarely, Logan came home for lunch. I had to be gone before that.

My parents were total assholes. Couldn't go there. I only had one place to turn.

Time to drive to Black Claw, Colorado.

Chapter 1 - Axel

The scent of peonies drove me wild as I stalked into the house with my mate in my arms. I'd known her all of thirty seconds, and already Asher was losing his shit. If he didn't calm down, he'd affect me more than he already was. Normally, I had no problem controlling my dragon, but we'd never met our fated mate before. This was a world unknown.

When I watched the car speed up the driveway and come to a stop in a cloud of dust in the middle of my nephew's shifting celebration, I'd done so with only a mild interest. My curiosity was slightly raised when I realized it was an extremely attractive friend of Ava's.

My police officer training had been kicked on when I saw her bruises, but none of that prepared me for the moment the wind shifted.

Asher had stirred as soon as she climbed out of her tiny red car. He sensed far before I did who she was to us. I was in the dark until her smell danced around us provocatively, ensnaring us in its grip with the lightest touch of a feather wrapped around a fist of iron.

Mate. We have a mate. She's our mate. Asher went so wild I nearly shifted right then, a problem I'd literally never had. As a beta dragon, Asher was predisposed to follow, to listen to reason.

He was still a dragon. Headstrong, willful, stubborn. He had a violent streak. But I'd always been able to control it. My human will was stronger than his.

Most of the time.

Today, it took everything I had, plus Zephyr, my alpha brother's dragon, to keep Asher in check.

When I'd seen her nearly collapse, wild dogs from hell couldn't have kept me from catching her. As soon as she was in my arms, Asher calmed somewhat. Until, as we walked in to the manor, he started worrying about her health.

She needs a human doctor.

I agreed with him. Rushing inside with Ava and pretty much our entire clan on my heels, Asher alternated between worry and rage.

Personally, I funneled my worry into rage. Whoever did this to her had to pay.

He must burn.

As a cop, I couldn't exactly set some dude on fire. However, I could use all my resources to see him brought to justice. I'd keep myself—and my dragon—far away from him as I did it.

Our oversized sofa was the closest place to lay her down comfortably.

She couldn't have come at a better time. Our entire clan was here for my nephew Maddox's first shift. He'd had his shift and we'd been just about to start the party—which normally would've lasted into well into the night—when Charlotte pulled up.

The clan doctor, Buddy, was here, which was a rare occurrence. He tended to stay near my grandfather's part of the clan because he held a much larger and more populated territory than my younger brother, our Alpha.

"Let me through." Buddy's voice cut through the worry and rage as he tried to get to Charlotte on the couch.

"Someone grab a warm cloth," my mother yelled. She was human, and my father was a beta, but I would've guaranteed three or more people jumped to do as she said. She had that sort of presence.

"Come on, Axel." Soft hands pulled me away from my mate. "Let Doc check her out."

I let Ava and Mom pull me away from Charlotte, even though that was the last thing I wanted to do.

Doc got on his knees beside Charlotte and began examining her. "I'll start with her vitals," he murmured.

He looked at her eyes with a little penlight and tutted. "I don't like how her eyes respond."

Asher grunted inside me, unhappy with that news. I held my breath and tried to stay back and not crowd the man.

Doc moved on to her blood pressure, pulling little machines out of a bag he'd produced. He wrapped a cuff around her wrist and pressed a button. The little blood pressure monitor whirred to life while Doc probed all over Charlotte's head.

All I wanted to do was cover Charlotte's body with my own and hold her.

That wouldn't help her in the slightest, though, so I let Ava's and Mom's touches help ground me.

Ava had quickly become very much the sister she'd been when we were kids. Maverick had never seen her that way, but to me she'd been a pesky little sister, tagging along with me and Mav, making us have to hide our true natures. I'd liked her, though, despite that. She had an undeniable charm.

"Ouch," he muttered. His hands moved around the back of her head, which he lifted off the couch and supported with one hand while exploring with the other. "Someone help me turn her, please."

I lurched forward to help, as did Ava and Mom. The three of us held her on her side at the edge of the couch while Doc used his penlight to examine the back of her head. My hands heated where they touched her thigh and the back of her knee, but I restrained myself. More than anything, I wanted to massage her legs, try to find some way to comfort her.

Claim her.

Not that. Not yet.

As soon as Doc parted her hair, the smell of her blood hit me. Gardenias mixed with copper.

We will kill the man who injured her.

Ignoring my dragon, I fought the same urges he had. We wouldn't kill him, but damn, it was hard not to promise my wild side that we would.

Doc tutted. "I opened the cut on her head with my exam." He finished exploring the wound on the back of her head and we let her rest again. I didn't get up this time. He could damn well explore around me.

"I'm going to perform a quick exam of her body. Please clear the room," Doc said. "Get a car to the door, she needs to go to the hospital, for sure. I'll give her a once-over to make sure we don't need an ambulance."

"I'll get my SUV." Ava jumped up and ran from the room.

"I'm not going anywhere," I said. My voice continued in a growl that I hadn't actually meant to let out.

"Son, nobody is asking you to leave. Just the general audience." Doc chuckled and looked over his shoulder.

For the first time, I glanced behind me. My entire clan was crammed in the entrance to the living room and front foyer, all of them trying to peer over each other's shoulders.

"You heard the man," I roared. "Get out!"

Even my grandfather, our clan's High Alpha, jumped a little at my tone. "Yep," he said. "Sounds like Axel's got this well under control." He spread his arms and turned away, ushering the rest of the family out the door, including my father and younger brother.

Ava ran back in, darting through the sea of the Kingston clan. "Car's right outside."

Doc waited for the room to empty down to just me, Ava, and Mom.

Maverick, my alpha and younger brother, stood in the foyer with his back to us, as if guarding us against anyone trying to come in. It was symbolic—nobody would dare bother us now that I'd made my feelings clear about the matter—but I appreciated him anyway.

"Okay, I need to examine her abdomen." He pulled up her shirt, and the mass of bruises on her stomach made me hiss as I sucked in a breath.

Asher lost his shit. I had to clench my fists around the cushions of the couch to keep him from making me physically upset.

Ava turned to look behind her at someone. "We need to call the cops."

"We are the cops, dear," Maverick responded.

"These are old. A couple of days." Doc pressed into her stomach and tutted again.

"If the bruises are old, it almost certainly didn't happen here," Maverick continued. "We need to contact the police from New Mexico and file a report."

Doc sat back on his heels. "Her liver is enlarged. It could be just how she's made, but I worry about internal bleeding." He stood with a pop of his lips, a worried sound. "This is beyond what I have with me, at least for a human. If she were a dragon, I could give her certain herbs and she'd heal herself. I could give her something for pain, but she needs a complete workup and body scans." He nodded his head toward her. "Take her to the car, Axel. Be gentle. She won't heal as fast as we do, and until you two bond, she's just a fragile human."

Just a fragile human. She'd been through a serious beating and had managed to drive all the way from New Mexico. She was anything but fragile.

And yet, I picked her up with the lightest possible touch. She moaned as I tucked her into my arms, stirring a bit, but not enough to talk to me.

"Ava," Doc said. I paused at the front door to listen to what he had to tell her. "Make sure they do a rape kit. These injuries are consistent with what we see with domestic violence. I could almost recreate the scene for you. There is often also rape in these situations."

Ava sucked in a shocked breath I heard clearly even in the next room. "Doc, if he raped her…"

"I know, dear. Wait for the test results and we will proceed then. It can't fall back on Axel, but we would handle it if it proves necessary."

They wouldn't have had to handle anything if her rape kit came back positive. There wouldn't be a force in the world that could've kept me from killing the man, and I had no idea who he was.

But I knew her name and what city she came from in New Mexico. That was enough.

I climbed carefully into Ava's backseat without putting Charlotte down. "Drive," I commanded as Maverick got in the front. He grabbed a light from the glove box and slammed it onto the top of the car. It was magnetic and plugged into the cigarette lighter. "I bought this for situations just like this, when we might need the SUV."

"We need to buy one for the department," I muttered as I looked down at the gorgeous woman curled up in my lap. She moaned or whimpered occasionally, making me want to wrap her tighter in my arms, but I didn't want to hurt her more.

Ava slid in beside me and took her friend's hand. "Hang on, Char. We got you."

The county hospital was a good half-hour drive from our house. Ava talked to Charlotte the whole way, nonsense stuff about being best friends and Charlotte staying with Ava.

I wanted to tell her I'd keep her safe and nobody would ever hurt her again, but couldn't bring myself to say the words in the car with my brother and his new mate.

When we pulled up to the hospital, several people in scrubs rushed out with a gurney. Mom had probably called ahead to let them know we were coming.

Two men I recognized as nurses from the times I'd been in the hospital on police business helped me lay Charlotte on the bed. They snapped up the metal rail sides and took off with her straight into a set of double doors just inside the entrance. I tried to follow, but a severe-looking woman wearing glasses on the end of her nose appeared with her hand up, blocking the doors as Charlotte disappeared around a corner. "Are you family?"

I shook my head.

"Next of kin? Spouse?"

With an internal roar of frustration that was all me, not Asher this time, I turned and stalked out of the emergency room doors. They wouldn't let me near her until she gave permission, and probably wouldn't tell me a word.

Maverick waited for me outside. Ava stayed in, and I watched her speak to the woman. They walked toward a row of desks behind windows—the reception area. Ava had Charlotte's purse in her hands.

"Ava will get her registered. She's her best friend, and the closest thing she has to family." Maverick put his hand on my shoulder.

My skin crawled with worry and anticipation. "What if he raped her?"

A beating was bad enough. But rape? How could she get past that? I'd do anything I could to help, of course, but she didn't know me yet. I couldn't fathom the emotional pain she'd go through if he'd raped her. Physical pain healed much faster than the scars an event like that would cause.

"Then we'll deal with it."

My skin rippled as the urge to shift nearly did me in.

Mom and Dad pulled up behind Ava's SUV, and Mom got out and rushed inside without a word to us as Dad walked over. "Anything?"

Maverick shook his head. "They just took her back. Ava's doing the paperwork, but I think he's about to lose it."

Dad nodded. "I figured. Come on, son. Let's get you home so you can shift."

I shook my head. "I'm not leaving her."

"She's not dying," Maverick said reasonably. "She's hurt, but not dying. Right?"

Even though I knew he was right, admitting it out loud meant leaving her. "She's not dying. I'd know."

Mates always knew. Though we weren't bonded, did that make a difference? I had no idea.

"Come on." Dad nodded his head toward the car. "You're doing her no good here freaking out. Go home, shift, process the fact that you have a mate, then come back and check on her."

I nodded, then fixed a glare on Maverick. "Keep me posted."

He smiled at me, sad but understanding. "Of course. I'll text you anything I hear. Anything at all."

He knew damn well the two things I wanted to know. That she was going to be okay and that she hadn't been raped.

I slammed the car door behind me after I got in and waited for Dad to hug Maverick and get in. "Come on, old man," I muttered. My skin rippled again as the worry, fear, and rage threatened to consume me.

Dad finally got in and turned us back toward our property. As soon as I knew we were on our land, still a good ten minutes from our house, I gripped the door handle. "Let me out."

Dad slammed on the brakes, and I launched out of the car, shifting as soon as I exited. My clothes ripped off of me, including my shoes. I did have a millisecond of regret; I loved those sneakers.

Then, Asher took over fully and all regrets left my head. I roared as I flew up the road, then up and over the trees. Pumping my wings, I headed farther and farther up the mountain, until the air grew thin and harder to breathe.

Asher didn't care about the thin air. It was soothing to a dragon, being in the cold air at the top of the mountain.

We owned the property for miles and miles around. I could fly for hours and not run into anyone who would be a danger to me. The wolf shifters of the area lived on the land as well, and they patrolled it frequently. Their sniffers worked even better than ours. If someone strange hit our land, we knew it well in time.

After flying up the mountain, I landed beside a stream for a drink. Asher's mind was at the forefront of our personality while we were shifted, though I did have the ability to force him to shift back if I needed to. He studied himself in the river's reflection in the fading light. It would be dark soon, and though I didn't mind flying in the dark, I wanted to see if there was any news of Charlotte.

This is not how I wanted to meet our mate.

Asher was not happy with the situation.

Neither was I.

As we flew toward home, I tried to reason with him. Hell, at least we'd met her. That was more than most dragons got. Fated mates were pretty rare, even for dragon shifters.

We couldn't wait to get to know her.

Chapter 2 - Charlotte

My head pounded until I woke up. Moaning, I covered my eyes. Why were all the lights on? They burned through my eyelids. Without opening them, I tried to roll over in bed and go back to sleep. No way I was getting up with a headache like this.

But I couldn't roll over. Something kept my arm from moving too far, and every time I tried, a tugging feeling made me stop.

Damn it. I didn't want to open my eyes, but what the fuck?

Cracking them, I held up one hand, the one that didn't feel weird, and squinted down at the arm that was acting up.

An IV stuck out of it. Why did I have an IV?

I hadn't been sick or anything, so why was I wearing a hospital gown and clearly lying in a hospital bed? I squinted and continued shading my eyes as I looked around. Ava was asleep in a chair beside my bed, her head leaned over on a pillow pressed against the handrail of my bed.

As my brain tried to clear, the pain set in. My head hurt the most, but even moving my head from side to side made my ribs hurt as well.

I tried to sit up and hissed as I realized just how sore my midriff was.

Memories flooded in then, of Logan hitting me, knocking me down. Had he kicked me? I couldn't remember. I'd gotten up and told him what he wanted to hear, doctoring myself as best I could and allowing him to feed me pain pills.

Oh, shit, had I driven to Colorado like that? The presence of Ava meant either I'd come to her or she'd come to me.

I tried to focus on the events of the last few days, but so much felt like sand slipping through my fingers. I couldn't recall much about the three days sleeping after Logan's beating, but I did suddenly remember packing everything I could fit into my Fiesta and hitting the highway. Had it been three days I'd stayed, waiting for the opportunity to leave? Maybe it was two.

Damn. I probably shouldn't have driven, especially not that far. But I'd made it.

Ava stirred and smiled at me.

"Hey, sleepyhead," I whispered. "What happened?"

"You passed out in my arms." She took my hand. "We were really worried about you."

I didn't ask who *we* was. Probably her kids and Maverick.

Tears filled her eyes as she stroked her thumb across my knuckles. "I was so worried," she whispered.

"You kept almost waking up and moaning in pain. It broke my heart."

With a chuckle, I squeezed her hand. "Stop. I'm okay."

She gave me a deadpan look.

"Well, I'm not *okay*, but I'll be fine. I'll get through this like I do every other breakup. With tequila and mint chocolate chip."

Ava snorted. "This is worse than anything I've ever seen you go through in a relationship."

She had a point there. I knew how to pick them, for sure. I'd had guys rough me up before, twice, but that was more like an intimidation factor. I'd let them know I wasn't someone they could easily bully or overwhelm, so they'd lost interest fast.

Not Logan, though. He'd hidden it well, waiting until I was moved in and we were all sweetly domestic to show his true colors. The bastard.

"Char, what happened?"

Her eyes pleaded with me to tell her, but I didn't want to. I had to explain how I ended up with yet another man that was toxic.

With a sigh, I told her all she needed to know. "Logan."

The tears spilled over and tracked down her cheeks. "I'm sorry."

"Nothing for you to apologize for." I looked away and out the window across the surprisingly large hospital room. "*You* didn't pick another complete loser."

She sighed and sat back. "You do know how to pick them."

That was the damn truth. I'd picked the wrong men time after time for my entire adult life. This one took the top prize, though. I'd never been beaten into the hospital.

"Char, I have to ask. Did he rape you?" She looked like she'd rather have asked me anything in the world but that.

"No!" I exclaimed. "He didn't. I promise." At least he'd given me that dignity. From the time he came home drunk, he didn't even ask me for sex.

Ava slumped in relief. "Thank goodness."

What did that say about me, that she'd been so worried I might've been raped? What did that say about the men I'd been seeing?

"I've got to make a change. You being so worried about me being raped says a lot about me," I whispered.

"No," she snapped. "It does not. It says a lot about men. Yeah, you always seem to go for the guy that isn't good for you, but we can work on that. Worrying that you might've been raped says a lot about *men.* Not you."

I burst into tears, grateful to my friend for recognizing my vulnerability. She climbed into the bed beside me and carefully put her arms around me. "We got this, Charlotte. You'll stay with me and Maverick and get on your feet. Don't worry."

Nodding my head, I rested it on her chest and tried to calm down. Maybe a move to Colorado would do me good. Get out of the city I grew up in, start over here where nobody knew me. Nobody knew my family or my history.

The door opened and an older man in a white coat came in. "Hello there," he said with a kind smile. "I'm Dr. Hamlish."

He held a tablet in his hand, rather than a clipboard. I guess the hospital in Black Claw had updated their technology. "You are a very lucky lady," he said. Tapping the screen, he showed me a picture from a cat scan. "You probably can't read that, but—"

"I can," I said.

"Sorry?" He'd been about to explain the picture to me and hadn't heard me.

"I can read it. I'm a nurse." I was proud of my degree and had even been considering going back for more.

"Oh, well, good then, here." He put the tablet in my hand. Ava climbed out of the bed so I could sit up properly. I winced as the movements sent shots of pain across my abdomen.

"You see here, your organs look great." He leaned over and flipped through several images, giving me a moment with each one to study the scans. "No internal bleeding. No broken ribs."

"How long was I out?" I asked. "If my injuries aren't that bad?"

"I didn't quite say not that bad," he said. "Just that you're lucky. You have a pretty nasty concussion, and that caused your bout of unconsciousness, which was roughly twelve hours, by the way. Your brain made your personality shut down and sleep so it could heal. How long ago did this happen?" He took the tablet back and tapped on it while I considered the question.

"So, this is Tuesday morning, then?" I indicated the window, where the sunrise had begun to brighten the room even with all the lights on.

Ava nodded. "You showed up late Monday evening. Last night."

"Friday night." Friday was when I'd made the dinner. My first day off. "Oh, no, I didn't call work."

"I did," Ava said. "I told them you wouldn't be back for a while, at least a week. Bought you time to figure out for sure what you want to do."

"Thank you." I studied my hands. No way I was going back to New Mexico, but I felt bad about leaving them high and dry. This whole situation was so damn embarrassing. How had I not realized what Logan was capable of?

"Well, you're clear to leave the hospital. You need lots of rest and don't do anything taxing. You might experience random headaches, moments of confusion or memory problems for weeks to come with a knock on the noggin that severe. You also might not. Either way, *take it easy.*" He smiled at me again. "Do you have somewhere you can rest up?"

Ava nodded eagerly. "She's staying with me as long as she needs to."

"Good. Don't let her do anything more strenuous than loading the dishwasher, and not even that for a few days." As he spoke, a nurse came around the bed and worked on removing my IV. I'd had them before, and put in a countless number of them at work. As usual, the worst part was removing the damn tape.

Ava saluted him. "Yes, sir."

"Charlotte," Dr. Hamlish said. "One last thing. I did not do a rape kit. We feel with your injuries it's necessary to ask."

I held up my hands. "It's okay. I know you had to ask, but no, he didn't rape me. A kit isn't necessary."

Dr. Hamlish nodded. "I'm glad to hear that. Very glad, young lady. Now, the next important thing. The police are outside and need to take a statement. Do you feel up to talking to them?"

I started to shake my head. Talking to the police and recounting every detail of what happened was the last thing I wanted to do. But Ava's eyes widened, then narrowed. If I said no, she might give me another concussion. Damn. "Yes. I'll talk to them."

I looked at my friend, the only person I'd had to turn to. "Will you stay with me?"

"Of course." Ava sat in the chair again and looked at the doctor. "Send them in."

One man walked in wearing street clothes. "Hello, dear. My name is James Kingston. You know Maverick?"

I nodded. "Of course."

"I'm his father. We are the police officers here in Black Claw, along with Maverick's brother Axel and a colleague of ours named Carlos. Due to the fact that your best friend is in a relationship with one of our officers, I'm obligated to offer to call in someone from the next county over to take your statement." His kind face put me at ease, even as he tried to tell me I didn't have to trust him. "However, it's not just an obligation. I want you to be the most comfortable you can be. This is a difficult process."

"It's okay. If he'd raped me, maybe I wouldn't want to talk to Maverick's dad." I chuckled ruefully. What a sad situation. "But he just beat the shit out of me, and you can take that statement all right."

James furrowed his brow and twisted his lips. "Okay. Why don't you start at the beginning? His name, your relationship to him and so on."

"Okay, well, his name is Logan. We met about six months ago at a singles party a mutual friend threw. He's in advertising." I wasn't really sure what else to say. I gave him Logan's address and phone number. "We dated for about five months before he asked me to move in with him. He'd been an absolute dream until then, so I did it, of course. Jump in with both feet, that's me."

I sighed and looked at Ava. I didn't want to recount the story of getting my ass beat.

"It's okay," Ava took my hand. "You can do this."

With my nerves running rampant, I closed my eyes and told them about the special dinner, the visit to the grocery store, and what happened after. When I finished telling them every single detail, I realized tears were coursing down my cheeks. It hurt more than I'd expected it to, telling them what Logan had done to me. Recounting the hits, the falls, the shaking.

The horrible three days I'd slept and pretended to be asleep if he came in the room.

"I can't ever see him again," I whispered. "Never again."

"You never have to," Ava said. "I'll make sure of that."

James makes a few notes on the pad of paper he'd used while I recounted my tale. "You're free to go," he said. "Please reach out if you think of anything else or if you need anything at all." He pressed a business card into my hand, patted Ava on the shoulder, and walked out.

"You ready to get out of here?" she asked.

"Beyond. I'm starving." My stomach growled as if to prove my point.

I threw my legs off the side of the bed, then groaned when my abdomen hurt from moving so fast.

"Easy does it," Ava said. She handed me my pants first, then when I groaned trying to bend over, she took them back and threaded my feet through the leg holes. She pulled them up enough for me to grab hold so I could hike them up as I stood.

The shirt was a little bit easier. "No, fuck the bra. I've got nice, perky tits. Won't kill anyone to see me without a bra."

Ava snorted and stuffed my bra into her purse. "Okay, gimme your feet and I'll put your socks and shoes on."

"You're a saint." I sat back down and watched her tie my sneakers. "Ready?"

"Yes." She held open the door for me to walk into the hall.

Walking wasn't too bad, so I did the best I could to move normally to the elevator.

"This way," Ava pointed me to the left, and I spotted an exit door.

When we hit the fresh air, Maverick smiled at us from his spot leaning on the side of Ava's SUV, and an incredibly handsome man stood beside him, staring at me intently.

"Hey, Charlotte. Glad to see you upright." He held open the back door for me. "Fancy a lift?"

"Thanks, Maverick." I walked toward the car, and the handsome man stuck his hand out.

"Hello. I'm Axel."

When I shook it, he only gripped lightly, as if afraid of hurting me. I had no idea why he was here with Maverick and Ava to get me, but at this point I didn't care. I just wanted to eat and lie down, though anyone else seeing me like this wasn't my favorite thing.

"Can we stop at the pharmacy?" Ava asked Maverick. "The doctor gave her some pain medicine."

"And food," I added. "I'm starving."

"Of course," Maverick said. "We only have a couple of fast food places in Black Claw. Do you want breakfast food or lunch food?" I didn't care and said as much. "Breakfast it is," Maverick replied.

He went to a drive-through and I got two breakfast burritos and a huge coffee. Moaning, I sucked down the scalding hot coffee. "Oh, that's good."

The ride was quiet and I ignored everyone and snarfed my food. When we got to the pharmacy, I cleaned up my mess and climbed carefully out of the SUV. "I'll be right back."

Damn, these small-town pharmacies didn't have a drive-through. I didn't feel like going in and everyone seeing me, but I had to give them my prescription and insurance information. They'd probably want ID.

"I'll go with you." Axel bounded from the back seat, where he'd sat beside me since we left the hospital.

He walked close and touched my elbow with the tip of his fingers. "Would you like to hold my arm?"

I looked into his gorgeous chocolate eyes and though I meant to say no, my head nodded yes. I was slightly unsteady still, after all.

He walked me to the pharmacy window and as soon as my hands hit the counter, he let go of me. At least he wasn't being overly touchy. As soon as I didn't need his support, he'd let go.

They had a twenty-minute wait.

"Come on. We'll get you home and I'll come back for it."

"Can they release narcotics to you?" I didn't want to get home then have to turn around and go back out, but now that I'd eaten, I wanted to lie down more than anything.

"Hey, Jim," Axel called to the pharmacist. "Can you release her script to me so I can take her home?"

The older man behind the counter looked up and nodded. "Sure. Since it's you."

"There." Axel looked supremely pleased with himself. "Let's get you home."

I sighed and let him help me back to the car. Within another quarter-hour, we pulled up to Ava's cabin.

"The kids are up at the manor," Ava said. "We'll have the house to ourselves for the rest of the weekend."

When I turned to open my door, Axel was already out of the car, around it, and opening the door for me. He held out a hand with a helpful smile and I accepted it gratefully.

"Ava's Maddox drove your car down and he and my brother took all your stuff in."

That was a relief. It was a car full.

He continued as we walked into the enormous cabin. "Our mom got your bags unpacked for you while you were at the hospital." He smiled tentatively. "She said to tell you she didn't mess with anything that looked too personal, not even your underwear. She just put a few clothes away, so you'd have something unwrinkled to wear."

That was lovely. I trusted Ava's judgment of the woman, and she'd told me before how much she trusted her. She must have because she let her kids around the woman constantly. That was nice that she'd gained grandparents for Hailey as well as Maddox.

Maddox was Maverick's son, but around the time Ava found out she was pregnant, Maverick had left town and she couldn't find him. They reconnected when Maddox was seventeen and Ava had another child, Hailey, from a previous marriage. Maverick and his family had absorbed Hailey like she was Maverick's. I loved them for that. Hailey was the sweetest child.

The stairs took me ages to get up. "I felt better than this yesterday," I grumbled. "Why do I feel so bad now?"

Axel kept holding out his hand as if to help or grab me and keep me from falling, but I wanted to make it on my own. "You were probably running on adrenaline. Were you still in the house with whoever did this yesterday?"

"Well, no. I was driving yesterday. But the day before I was, and I felt horrible, but not this bad." I felt comfortable talking to him for some reason, even though I barely knew him.

He nodded as we topped the stairs. "Yep, probably adrenaline. You'll be able to rest now, and heal."

We walk into the same bedroom I'd used when I visited before. "Here you go."

I wondered why Ava hadn't walked me up, but Axel was nice, so I didn't complain. He was nice to look at, too, but that was beside the point.

"Listen, Charlotte." I turned back to him to see him looking nervous. "I'm one of the police officers in Black Claw, and I live just up the road. The house you first came to when you got here, that's my home. If you ever need anything, just yell. Or call. Ava has my number so you can put it in your phone."

He pulled the door nearly closed. "Stick with us, Charlotte." I liked the way he said my name. He put a little lilt on the vowels. "We'll keep you safe."

He shut the door. I looked around the room at my bags and boxes, everything from my car, but the bed was too inviting to begin thinking about unpacking. I collapsed on the bed, waking only long enough to take one of the pills Ava put to my lips. I had nothing to think about but Logan and six wasted months of my life. Crying softly, I fell asleep as the effects of the pill took hold, drifting into a dream where Axel kept trying to tell me something, but I was too upset to listen.

Chapter 3 - Axel

My patrol was almost over, thank goodness. Every time I turned around, I found my cruiser moving closer and closer to Ava's place. The town was having a sleepy Friday, most people staying home in the early spring chill. It wasn't warm enough for the drive-in theater to open, and the only place the kids liked to hang out was a local diner, which only offered a limited menu in the winter.

We were technically in spring, but the cold hadn't quite let up. The days were fairly warm, but not the nights.

With a sigh, I turned around after realizing I was halfway back to the road that led up to Ava's cabin and my parents' manor house.

Charlotte was burned in my mind, a now-permanent fixture of my psyche. I hadn't seen her since the day I helped her to her room, but that didn't mean I'd stopped thinking about her. Not for a second.

Asher had wanted me to take her on the bed right then, but of course, that hadn't even remotely been an option. I wouldn't violate her trust for all the money in the world.

Dragons were sexual beings. They wanted to express all their emotions with sex. Feeling protective? Have sex. Sad? Sex would cheer him up. Angry? Have some angry sex.

Luckily, I had more sense than that. Charlotte would sleep with me when she was damn good and ready and not a moment before. She'd take the lead with the physical side of our relationship. It was the best way to build trust with her. She had to trust me with her life before I could tell her the truth or else she'd spook and run.

No, I had to go about this the right way.

Driving aimlessly, I watched the clock on the dash tick toward four, when I could go back to the station. At least there I could sit at a desk and contemplate Charlotte instead of doing it driving around town where I could easily head in her direction. Patrol shifts were normally fun. I'd stop in and check on different businesses, say hi to people, and generally spend the time socializing.

Not this week. I just wanted to drive somewhere closer to Charlotte. I had to give her space.

Even Asher was committed to giving her all the time she needed, but it was so damn hard to stay away. Her scent lingered in my mind like a siren song, transfixing me.

We are Maverick's brother. We can be at the cabin.

It was true, we could hang out at the cabin, but it might weird Charlotte out. I didn't want to add anything troubling to her already fragile life. She'd had a rough time of it and deserved the space.

Finally, the clock gave me permission to head back to the station. I went in and relieved Carlos, who had been on desk duty and would now take over patrol. When he got back at eight, then I'd go home and our probie, Jordyn, would come in for the night shift. I settled in to organize my desk. I had no paperwork to do, and Carlos had cleaned the station, dusting and sweeping. We had no prisoners at the moment, either. Black Claw was generally the best place to be a police officer. We stayed somewhat uneventful, which was always good, if somewhat boring at times.

Three-quarters of the way through my shift, my baby brother Jury and nephew Maddox burst through the doors, laughing and grinning. They held several Tupperware containers I recognized as belonging to my mother.

"Excellent. Dinner?" My mother sent dinner to me when I worked this shift. Sometimes she delivered it, sometimes she sent another member of the family. I knew she sent lunch frequently as well, but we were more likely to stop and pick up a sandwich somewhere during the day than go out for dinner.

Jury nodded. "Yep. Mom sent us. Said you'd forget to eat if we didn't feed you, so here we are."

They set the containers on Maverick's desk and unpacked a canvas bag. She'd put in plates, napkins, silverware, the whole kit. That was the way she was, remembering every detail.

"She knows we have all this stuff here." I laughed and shook my head.

Maddox held out a plate. "Don't fight it. She said we're to stay while you eat, bring back the dishes and leftovers and not leave anything you'd have to clean up here." He wiggled the plate in front of me. She hadn't even sent paper plates and plastic cutlery. She sent the real stuff and would wash it as soon as the guys took it back.

With a snort, I took the plate and began peeking into the containers. "Well, by all means then. You can't disobey Mom. She's a bear when pissed."

"I haven't seen her mad," Maddox said. "She can't be that bad." He looked pretty skeptical, but if he'd never seen it, I understood his confusion. My mother was a small, quiet woman…until she got mad. Then she turned into a whole different kind of dragon.

Jury and I burst into laughter and Jury elbowed Maddox in the ribs. "She's terrifying."

Maddox shook his head in disbelief. He'd learn one day. One of us would piss Mom off enough and Maddox would see. Then he might run for the hills.

But who knew? He was her first grandchild. She might be different with him.

Jury was born a few months before Maverick and Ava conceived Maddox, so they were pretty close in age. Now that Maddox was about to graduate high school, they were talking about their futures and what they want to do with their lives.

Jury already graduated nearly two years before, but he was special. He had to stay close to the family due to his rare ability to track. If other clans learned we had a tracker, they'd either try to kill him or steal him. Neither was an option. He hadn't been happy about not being able to go away to college, but eventually, he'd given in. The danger was too great to have him away from his clan. At best he could've gone to stay with our grandfather, the High Alpha of our clan, but he'd opted to stay at home.

He wanted to be a forest ranger, though, and had found an online college to take wildlife and ranger classes. I was so proud of him. He worked hard, much harder than I did at his age. All I did was goof off and try to skip classes. I'd taken classes in Arizona after we moved from Black Claw to be near my grandfather.

Living at home and so close to his nephew also meant Jury got to be a kid for a while longer, which was nice. He enjoyed goofing off with Maddox, but that didn't mean I missed the time he spent studying and working on his classes.

He was a damn good kid.

I dug into the chicken and potatoes mom sent, piling the mixed roasted veggies high on my plate. Maddox and Jury sat at Maverick's desk and spun the chairs around. "Are you two really going to sit around and pester me until I'm done eating?" I took a big bite of chicken. "Mmm, this is good. Feel free to dig in."

As usual, Mom had sent enough for an army when it was only me here tonight. I'd make a plate for Carlos and put it in the microwave and still, there'd be leftovers to send back to the house.

"We ate at home," Jury said. "It's Friday night and Black Claw has nothing going on, so here we are." They looked bored to tears. I snickered and remembered how frustrating it was to be their age and bored. They probably wanted to run far away to find some fun.

As I ate, as usual, my mind drifted back to Charlotte. It had been almost a week since she'd driven into my life. I'd managed to stay away the entire time, but my patience was wearing thin. I needed to see her, just lay eyes on her.

"What are the odds that my Uncle Axel would end up with my Aunt Char?" Maddox mused as he spun in his chair. "That's pretty cool, both parts of my life colliding like that." He'd been raised with a stepfather in New Mexico. When Ava was barely pregnant, Maverick had been close to his first shift. An Alpha's first shift was volatile, and Maverick's was no exception. He'd lost his temper and beat a young, cocky dragon in our town nearly to death. We'd gotten out of town after that, disappearing without a trace. We were with my grandfather's clan, using my mother's maiden name, but Ava didn't know that. She'd raised Maddox all on her own until she met his dirtbag stepfather.

Now they were back and back together. It had all worked out in the end. And with Ava came Charlotte, my fated mate. If we hadn't moved away, Ava never would've moved back to New Mexico with her son, never would've met Charlotte, and I never would've met my mate. Amazing the paths life took.

"Well, it's true. There's no way I can deny it now after you all saw the way I reacted to meeting her the first time." I really wished I'd handled it better and kept cool. She deserved to be the third one to know that we were mates, the first two being me and Asher. But now my entire clan knew, and they all waited with bated breath to see how our story would unfold.

Great. Nothing like an audience. Especially a gossiping, interfering audience like a big pack of dragons.

"Jury and I have decided to be bachelors forever," Maddox said with a puffed-out chest. "Mates are too complicated and bring too many problems."

I snorted into my potatoes. "Okay." Whatever they wanted to believe.

Dragons didn't always have fated mates, but we were social creatures. We wanted to settle, find a home. That's why rogue or nomad clans were so rare. One dragon might have a stint in life of going rogue or going nomad, but they didn't do it very long.

We needed roots, family. A clan. And that usually meant a mate. It was something we couldn't fight, a part of our dragon sides that pushed us, motivated us.

Going so long without meeting anyone, after leaving Arizona and who I'd thought would be my mate, Jenna, had left me feeling bereft. Like I'd never find someone to spend my life with. It was a terrible feeling.

Jenna and I had tried the long-distance thing for a while, but it never worked. We ended up arguing, missing calls, and generally feeling miserable. Finally, we'd agreed a clean break was necessary.

Now I knew why. I was meant to be with Charlotte. Some higher power that I didn't understand had put our paths together and we'd live our best lives in each other's company.

Fated mates *could* resist the pull, but I'd never heard of any that wanted to. Finding a perfect mate was a dream come true for most. Those who resisted were reported to never find true peace, never have true contentment.

Maddox fixed me with a stare and arched an eyebrow. "I heard Mom and Aunt Char talking. Char is having a rough time. She's been having nightmares about that asshole that beat her. Mom told her she thinks she has PTSD, but Char wouldn't listen."

He and Jury went on to talk about PTSD, but my mind was glued to Charlotte. She was in pain. What if knowing I would do anything to protect her would help her feel safe again? I should've told her more clearly than just offering assistance that night in her room. I would've done anything to protect her. Down to laying down my life. Even though we'd just met, it was instinctual. I had to protect my mate.

There was nothing that said I couldn't be her friend, though. She was going through some serious trauma, and though being there for her as her mate wasn't possible, I could be the guy next door. Get to know her a little in a platonic way. At least then I could check on her.

I had to do *something*, anything without making it worse for her.

On the way home, I stopped at the grocery store, making it just before they closed at eight. I'd had to hightail it out of the station five minutes early to get there, but I made it. "I just need two things, I'll be fast," I told the cashier, who looked very irritated that I was coming in under the wire.

The ice cream was in the back of the store, but I jogged, grabbed three flavors, then swung through the produce department to grab a bouquet of flowers—not much of a selection in such a tiny grocery store, but it would do. They were bright and colorful and still perky, so I was happy with them. It wasn't the right time for roses, anyway. Not yet.

The cashier rang it up quickly, and I set out for Ava's place before the ice cream melted.

Hailey answered the door. "Mom! It's Uncle Axel!" She gave me a quick hug, then took off deeper into the house, unconcerned with my visit.

Ava walked out of the living room with Maverick on her heels. "Hey, Axel, how are you? What are you doing here?"

I shrugged. "Fine. Here." After shoving the bag of ice cream and the flowers into her arms, I stuffed my hands in my pockets. "There's enough ice cream for everyone, but I didn't know what flavor she liked, so I got three different kinds. You don't have to tell her who brought the stuff, just that someone was thinking about her." I knew I was rambling, but it kept me from running up the stairs to find Charlotte.

Ava handed the stuff over to Maverick and threw her arms around me. I patted her on the back while Maverick watched bemusedly. She clung to my neck. I was pretty sure she was trying to comfort me. The only thing that would comfort me was the sight of Charlotte, but I wouldn't even ask.

"I know this is hard on you," Ava whispered in my ear. "I know what it was like for Maverick before he could tell me the truth and Charlotte is in a much worse place than I was." She finally let go of me.

I rubbed the back of my neck. She'd hugged me hard. "I just hope they lift her spirits for a few minutes."

"I appreciate you not trying to bulldoze your way in." Ava shot Maverick a consternated look. He probably deserved it. He was a bulldoze through life kind of guy.

I was more of a strategically plan for my next move sort. "She'll have all the time she needs. I'll be here waiting for her when she's ready." Waiting and agonizing the whole time, but shit, I'd be there.

After giving them both a nod of my head as a goodbye, I headed to the car and up to the manor. Mom tried to feed me again, and I wasn't able to escape until I tried some of her blackberry cobbler. It filled me up, so I headed off to bed figuring I'd fall asleep fast with a full stomach after a long day of being bored at work.

No such luck. I tossed and turned, the same way I had all week, thinking about Charlotte. What she was like, what she enjoyed doing, what she hated. What foods did she like? Did she want kids? Did she like cats or dogs more?

I couldn't wait to learn more about her and get to know her. That would be when I could get some peace and sleep.

Sighing, I rolled over and prepared to spend another long night alone in my bed.

Again.

Chapter 4 - Charlotte

"It's been a week." Ava set a plate of pancakes down in front of me. I wasn't sure where the kids were, but it was nearly noon. I'd been sleeping pretty late.

Thankfully, Ava hadn't given me a lot of grief about it. She'd been the perfect friend the entire week, giving me all the space I needed. "I know." I dug into my pancakes, ravenous.

If I'd learned nothing else this week, it was that I definitely eat my feelings. Why couldn't I have been one of those women that can't eat a bite when stressed?

"Where is your head at?" She sat beside me and sipped a cup of tea.

With a sigh, I contemplated her question. "It's not great, Ava." I'd been thinking about talking to her, anyway. She'd given me a solid week before trying to make me talk.

It seemed fair to me. "I'm having nightmares. Vivid, anxiety-inducing… They're so real."

"About the beating?" Her voice lowered with concern.

"Yeah. It's not always the same. But I'm always in pain and terrified." Shoveling more food into my mouth, I washed it down with the coffee Ava had prepared with the perfect amount of cream and sugar. "And then I can't get back to sleep for a long while after. I'm not actually sleeping around the clock, but it seems like it, I guess."

"Have the nightmares gotten any better?" Ava put her hand on my arm. "Maybe you should talk to someone."

"I thought about that." Sipping the coffee with my best friend's comforting hand on my arm was the safest and most comfortable I'd felt for the entire week. "I'm not against it." I didn't tell her how weak it made me feel to contemplate the *need* for therapy. I should've been able to move past this on my own.

It wasn't like I'd lived with the man for years. We weren't even totally in love. The cohabitation had worked for us. We were in hardcore lust, sure. I cared about him, yeah. But head over heels deeply in love? Nah.

I had hoped he was the one, though. But I'd learned by then not to hold my damn breath. I knew time would tell, and right up until that moment, I'd been happy with what time was telling me.

Then, he came home drunk and was a completely different person. A dark, jealous, abusive person.

If he was willing to hurt me that bad after six months, what would he have done at a year, or five years, or a decade? By then, I might've been dead.

No, thanks. Not this bitch.

What I'd attributed to passion had been rage simmering under his surface. I'd called his sadism stubbornness and opinionated.

I was a blind fool. A weak, blind fool.

"Has he called?" I had zero desire to speak to him, but I was curious if he'd even tried to find me.

"I don't know. I turned your phone off once you called work."

I'd hated telling them I wouldn't be back, but it was for the best.

After a few days of nightmares and feeling so low, I'd considered up and leaving. I had a little bit saved up—thank *goodness* we hadn't combined our money—and I could afford to start over somewhere new. It would wipe me out, but it was doable.

But leaving Ava felt like a blow that would put me over the edge. My friend was all I had left. My shitty family certainly didn't care where I was or what I did.

"Start by looking it up. You can use my office. Look up testimonies of other women who have been through it. Maybe you can find an online support group." Ava stood and took my empty plate. "And build up to a therapist if you're on the fence about it." I listened to the sounds of her washing the dishes in the sink.

She had a dishwasher, but it was already running. I should've stood and done them myself, but I'd learned early on she'd have no part of that.

"Today, we're getting out of the house." She shut the water off with a snap.

I turned in my chair to watch her dry her hands. "I'm still bruised."

The black eye had faded to a green and yellow hue, but that would stick around for a couple of weeks. Ava touched my chin, lifting my gaze upward and studying my eye in the light. "Concealer will cover it. Besides, we're only going up to the manor."

My eyes widened, and my nerves jingled. "The manor?"

That was Maverick's parents' house. And his brothers'.

"Yep. Carla is doing a big barbecue. The party got cut short the other night. Most of the clan is gone, but she wanted to celebrate Maddox a bit more."

My heart pounded. I was the reason the celebration was canceled. I'd rolled up and passed out in the middle of them celebrating Maddox. "What were you celebrating anyway?"

Ava hummed and turned to hang the towel up. "Oh, just Maddox graduating soon. An early party."

It was a damn early party. He still had several months till graduation. "I'm sorry. The party was cut short because of me."

She waved me off, swatting me with the towel she'd almost hung up. It hit my butt like a feather. "Make up for it by coming today."

I couldn't refuse her, no matter what I wanted to do. Hiding in my room sounded much better, maybe binge-watching something online. But Ava had dropped everything to help me. I'd go to the barbecue.

"Well, let me go see if I can cover this shiner. If I can, I'm in."

My ribs and torso were still sore, but the doc said nothing was broken, so it sure could've been much worse. We'd just gotten through Christmas, which Logan and I had spent together, ignoring both of our families. I wouldn't have gone to mine no matter what, and Logan had said his family was too much drama for a new relationship.

I'd understood, but now I wondered if he hadn't been protecting me from them. Maybe he was hiding me, afraid they'd let something about him slip.

As I applied several layers of makeup, I pondered it. I'd never met a single member of his family, not even over the phone. I'd seen plenty of pictures and met some of his friends, but for the most part, it had just been me and Logan.

Should've freaking seen it. Damn it.

I sighed and twisted my body on the little vanity chair in my room as I worked on my face. The ache had lessened over the last couple of days especially. I took anti-inflammatory medicine around the clock as well. That had a lot to do with it. Normally, I stayed away from any medicine. Then if I truly needed it, like now, it worked well.

The makeup looked okay. Out in the bright sun, it would look a little heavy, but this time of year, surely we'd be inside.

My hair was easy, thankfully. My mother hadn't given me much good in life, but she'd given me her hair. Thick, blonde, with just enough waves to curl if I wanted and straighten if I wanted. If I left it alone, it was what the online bloggers called beachy waves.

I had a tendency to gain weight and my pores were way too big, but at least I had good hair. Shaking it out, I gave it a spritz and sighed at my reflection. Too pale, too wan. I felt like a country mouse, and that wasn't me at all.

Coming back to myself after such a traumatic event was damn hard. But I'd get there. I was determined.

I picked out a cute sweater and jeans. One of the few things I'd done over the past week was unpack. Ava had made it clear that I was welcome here for as long as I needed it. She'd told me she expected me to be here months, maybe longer.

One day, I'd repay her kindness, somehow.

But for now, baby steps. I smoothed the soft sweater over my stomach and ignored the tender spots. The jeans were more like jeggings, so they didn't push against my stomach but still looked cute tucked into my boots, which were also comfortable.

When I got downstairs, Ava was ready to go as well.

"Where's Maverick?" I asked.

"He took a morning shift. Their deputy, Carlos, is taking the afternoon so everyone can be at the celebration. They've got a probie, too, but they only leave him alone at night when the town is all asleep. Around here, that's the least eventful time, thank goodness."

Nothing like the city. The cops all hated the night shift in the city. It was the craziest time with the most complications.

"I guess I'm ready."

Ava took my hands and studied my face. "You look great. Did you contour?" She squinted. "I can't contour."

Laughing, I squeezed her hands. "I'll show you. If you can get it right, it's gorgeous, but so many people do it wrong and look like zebras."

We walked to her SUV hand-in-hand. "We'll walk another time. It's cold and you're still sore."

We laughed about makeup all the way up the long driveway to the manor. It came into sight with a snow-covered roof. The home was enormous, with multiple stories. High-set windows indicated it even had a big attic.

"I wonder if it has secret passages," I whispered as we parked. Peering straight up, I couldn't see the top of the house from the inside of the car. She'd parked too close to the front door.

Following her lead, I got out and looked at the piles of snow to the side of the driveway where they'd shoveled it away. Ava went to the back of the car and opened the trunk to reveal all kinds of goodies. "I didn't know this was in here." I laughed as I took in all the food.

Two cardboard boxes loaded with plastic containers filled up the back of the SUV. She grabbed one.

I leaned in to get the other, but she slapped my hand. I jerked it back and raised my eyebrow at her, relieved that her action hadn't caused me to flinch. That had to be a good thing.

"Oh, gosh, I'm so sorry. I didn't mean to smack at you." She set the box back down and hauled me into a hug as the front door opened. "I didn't want you to pick it up and aggravate your injuries."

Grimacing, I tried to wiggle out of her guilty embrace. "You're hurting me more than the slap did."

She released me with a squeal and covered her mouth with her hands. "I'm messing it all up."

Laughing, I took her hand and pulled her toward the door. "You're not. Come on."

Maddox and Jury, who I'd met on my visit before, stood on the porch. "Need help?"

"Get the boxes?" I asked. If I couldn't carry anything, neither could she.

"Yes, ma'am." Jury saluted me and bounded down the stairs. I moved much slower upward and cursed his youthful vigor, then remembered I was just as bouncy when

I wasn't half-beaten. I forgave him before we got to the top of the stairs.

Maverick's mom met us at the door. "Hello, welcome!" Carla had a friendly, open aura about her. She scooped me from Ava's grasp and put her arm around me as she led us in the house. "I'm so glad you came. We didn't think you would."

We walked into a foyer full of beautiful, dark wood. A lone table in the center held a bouquet of flowers that had to have been grown in a hothouse this time of year. They reminded me of the ones that Ava had put in my room. She'd said they were from Maverick's brother, to brighten my day, but hadn't said which one.

I assumed the older brother. Nineteen-year-old Jury didn't seem the type to think to send flowers or ice cream, which I'd enjoyed that evening with the company of the flowers and a TV show about solving crimes by studying bones.

"Now, you sit here and talk to everyone while I get the rest of the food together. We barbecued out back, but this cold snap has us inside to eat." She let go of me at the couch. I had no choice but to sit beside James, Maverick's dad.

Maverick walked in with his older brother, Axel. He was the one that had gone to the pharmacy for me. A real gentleman, that one.

"Hello, young lady," James said. "Nice seeing you upright." He patted my knee in a very fatherly way.

"It's nice to be upright. I've spent the last several days recuperating." No sense in lying, even if I did cover my bruises.

"Well, you look like a million bucks." He cut his eyes around the room. "Don't let my wife hear me say that." He winked and stood, ambling over to Ava, who followed her son into the room giving instructions for the food. "There's my gorgeous daughter," James said with his arms out.

He wasn't creepy, not at all. More like he felt himself the father of the group. And he was. Immediately upon talking to him, I felt like he was happy to have me there as a part of his family's celebration.

Maddox and Jury disappeared through the far door Carla had gone through. When it swung open, I caught sight of a kitchen and heard Hailey's girlish giggle. I'd assumed she was here. Ava said she had a hard time getting her out of Carla's grasp these days.

She complained, but I knew how thrilled she was for Hailey to have a grandmother in her life again. Ava's mom was as bad as mine. Maybe worse. And her Nana had passed away before Hailey was born.

Even though Hailey wasn't Maverick's biological child, the entire family treated her as if she was. A chosen family often ended up better than a biological one, anyway. The little girl was lucky.

Maverick hugged Ava, whispering in her ear while her face reddened. I grinned and ducked my head, looking at the coffee table. It felt weird not to be up and talking to everyone. Usually, I was the life of the party, but I just didn't have it in me at the moment. I'd be better off on the sidelines today. A few magazines spread across the top caught my eye. As I reached for one, someone sat on the couch beside me.

"Nice to see you again," Axel said in a low voice. "You look well."

With him sitting right next to me, it would be rude not to look him in the eye, so I turned my knees toward him. I didn't want to turn my torso or neck; it was still too uncomfortable.

Looking him dead in the face, I nearly sighed. Good Lord, the man was gorgeous. I'd been in such a bad place when I left the hospital, I wasn't sure I'd gotten a good look at him then and we'd never gotten around to actually meeting when I'd visited Ava previously.

His brown eyes twinkled under black eyelashes long enough to make any woman jealous. I'd spent ten minutes getting my lashes to look half that good.

Smiling, I went into flirt mode automatically, but my heart wasn't fully in it.

No straight woman in her right mind could sit next to this man without straightening her spine and sticking her boobs out a little.

But that hurt my ribs, so after a few seconds of it, I relaxed again. "Thank you. I'm a little sore and bruised still, but nothing a little concealer couldn't hide." There. Now maybe he wouldn't think I always wore this much makeup caked on. I lowered my eyelashes. "You look well yourself."

What the hell was I doing? *Shut it down, you idiot.* I was in no position to flirt, especially with Ava's fiancé's brother. My mind was freaking broken. I'd launched straight into flirt mode without thinking about it.

I had to start doing better for myself. If I got into another relationship, it would be with slow, confident progress. Not flirting with the first hot guy to bat his mile-long eyelashes at me.

"How are you liking Colorado?" Axel asked. He adjusted his position on the couch, opening up the space between us. Not moving away, but showing he wasn't trying to be up in my bubble. A respectful move.

"I haven't had much chance to see it. I will soon, though. Especially when the weather changes. I'd like to hike, explore the countryside."

He nodded and his eyes lit up. "That was part of the reason that helped me decide to move back when my family did. I could've stayed in Arizona, but I missed the

mountains. I love being outside. Hiking, swimming, fl—"
He cut off with a cough. "Oh, excuse me. Something in my
throat."

Before he coughed, I'd found myself enchanted by
his voice. "No problem. So, you're outdoorsy?" I wanted
him to keep talking. His rich, smooth voice had an odd
calming property to it. I found my nerves soothed.

He went on, talking about camping in the mountains
and all the land his family owned. His words revealed a
thankfulness for his good fortune that I didn't think he
realized. He wasn't a snotty rich boy. He was truly grateful
that his family had this good fortune.

"Has anyone ever mentioned how soothing your
voice is?" I'd interrupted him, so rude. "I'm so sorry." I
covered my mouth. "I interrupted you."

"No, it's okay. I was talking too much. But no, I
don't believe I've heard that before, that I have a soothing
voice." He cocked up one corner of his mouth, revealing a

dimple in the middle of his slight beard growth. I couldn't tell if he just hadn't shaved in a few days or if he always kept a scruff. It wasn't quite enough to be a beard, though it was even enough that I was sure he could grow one if he wanted to.

"You could do ASMR work if you wanted." I nodded and pursed my lips to emphasize my surety.

He laughed. "I don't even know what that is."

I tried to explain, but I just made him even more confused. "I'm trying to remember what it stands for." It was on the tip of my tongue. "Something sensory something response." He must've thought I was a lunatic. I laughed and tried to redeem myself. "It's inducing euphoria just by the tone of your voice."

Before I could go deeper into explaining—because, by the expression on his face, he thought I was nuts—Carla walked in.

"Soup's on!" She grinned at me and Axel, and I realized we were alone in the living room. I hadn't realized Ava and Maverick had walked out.

Axel jumped up and offered me his hand. I took it gratefully and let him help me stand. "Thanks. It's still a little painful."

"I've bruised my ribs before." He let go of my hand as soon as I was upright. "It sucks."

I nodded and laughed, regretting the laughter, because it twinged through my abdomen. "That's an understatement."

He held the door open for me. Carla had the food spread out across the kitchen island, and it looked like enough to feed an army. But, as Maddox and Jury piled up two plates each, I realized it was only enough to feed a house full of men.

Axel stepped in front of me, taking two plates as well. He dished a few pieces of barbecue ribs onto one plate.

As I reached for my own, he looked at me with the tongs held out. "Ribs?"

"Sure, just a little," I replied, shocked. The second plate wasn't for him. It was for me.

He placed a small slab on my plate, then picked up a serving spoon in a bowl of macaroni and cheese. After putting a scoop on his plate, he looked at me with eyebrows raised.

"A lot, please." I giggled. "I love that stuff." It looked like it had been baked, which was the best.

He put an enormous serving on my plate. He repeated the process, dishing something for himself then checking to see if I wanted some for green beans, potato salad, corn on the cob, and broccoli casserole. When he asked if I wanted okra, I had to refuse. "No, thank you."

"I'll just eat your share, then." He put a second scoop on his plate. "You don't know what's good."

Oh, he wanted to be like that. "Says the man that didn't take any green beans. Those are Italian cut. The best."

"Thank you," Carla called from the table. She stood behind Jury and Maddox, handing out napkins. "I don't know why that boy won't eat green beans!"

We moved to the table, and Axel set my plate across from Maddox, then his own plate beside mine. "Soda, tea, water?"

"Water, please." No sense in drinking my calories. I'd have water and not feel guilty about dessert.

I sat down while he got drinks. When he was seated beside me, I touched his hand with the tip of my fingers and he jumped as if I'd shocked him, but he didn't pull away, so I didn't worry. "Thank you." Butterflies erupted in my stomach when I touched him.

"No problem. I figured it would be easier than you having to hold the plate. I've had hurt ribs, I told you. Just dishing out some mac-n-cheese can be painful."

He was right, but I had to get myself under control. I had no place fighting butterflies right now. Being attracted to someone this hot off of a relationship with such an explosive ending was a nightmare waiting to happen.

Some of the family still stood at the island, filling their plates, but I noticed Jury, Maddox, and Axel were eating, so I dug into my food instead of speaking any more. Carla set a napkin beside me just after I bit deeply into the buttery corn. "Fank you," I mumbled.

Geez, these people were going to think I was raised in a barn. I swallowed the bite, blotted my lips, and thanked her properly. "Thank you for the napkin, and especially for inviting me today. This is nice."

Everyone eventually sat, and we talked and laughed. Well, they did. I observed, still feeling shy. It didn't take me long to realize Axel did more observing and chuckling than interacting. I wondered why that was. He was comfortable, and a loved member of the family.

He was nothing like the men I usually dated. They were flashy, charismatic. Usually loud and showy. Axel was quiet, dignified. He had a comforting presence.

Not long after I finished my food, my head pounded a couple of times. That wasn't the best sign. The concussion hadn't given me too many symptoms. I hadn't been confused or anything, but I'd had several nasty headaches since leaving the hospital. They always started with a few pounds of pain, then a few more, then slowly they escalated to enough pain to warrant a bigger pain pill and a nap.

Ava had sat on the other side of Axel. I leaned forward. "I think I need to get home. I feel one of those headaches coming on," I whispered. "I'm so sorry." I knew she planned to be there for hours more. "If you'll take me down, you can come right back."

I would've offered to walk, but it was damn cold, and if the headache escalated too fast, the walk would be torture.

Axel couldn't help but overhear what I said, considering I said it over his lap. "Let me take you," he offered. "Ava can stay here."

"No," Ava said. "I don't mind."

Axel shook his head. "I insist."

Ava's eyes sparkled as she agreed. "You better take good care of her."

He clapped his hand over his heart. "Like she was my own mate."

Mate. What an odd way to phrase it. But at least he made me feel comfortable. And Ava wouldn't have let me go anywhere with someone unless she trusted them with her life. And I trusted her with mine, which meant that trust transferred to Axel.

"Thank you," I said. Grabbing my plate, I turned to at least put it in the sink. "Carla, I'm so sorry. I had planned to offer to do the dishes, but I think I need to lie down."

She rounded the table and took my plate. After setting it in the sink, she pulled me into her arms. "Sweet girl, what do you think I had all these boys for? They'll do the dishes." She squeezed me with a gentle touch and pulled away. "I wouldn't have let you do them, anyway."

I kept thanking them and waving goodbye until I realized Axel had maneuvered me out a different door. This one didn't lead to the living room, but straight back out into the foyer. I hadn't even noticed this door when we came in.

"We'll take Ava's SUV since it's right up front," he said. "Did you wear a coat?"

I shook my head. "Not since we weren't going far." My sweater was nice and thick. I figured I'd be fine, and I had been.

"No problem. Stay here. I'll start the car."

I looked around the foyer as I waited, but he was only gone seconds. My head wasn't any worse, just the occasional pound of dull pain.

"Ready?" He shut the front door behind him and held out a hand.

I let him hold my hand down the stairs, feeling a little unsteady. Damn this concussion.

"I'm sorry," I said as he got in the driver's seat. He had shut the door for me but hadn't pushed it so far as buckling my seatbelt. Chivalry without being creepy. The man was too damn attractive.

"Don't be sorry. You're healing from a traumatic injury. This stuff is bound to happen."

He drove at a snail's pace down the driveway. "I don't want to bump you."

Damn him. He had to have a flaw. "You're very considerate," I commented.

He didn't respond, but when we pulled into Ava's driveway and parked beside the snowdrift, he bounded out of the car and opened my door, holding his hand out.

"I'll walk you in."

She'd left the front door unlocked. "Does she have a key?" I asked.

He looked at the keys in his hand. "Yep. There's one here."

That made me feel a little better. "Good, because I can't leave the door unlocked."

"I'll go check the back door." He left me alone in the hallway and headed to the kitchen. "Yep," he said when he returned. "Locked. Lock this one behind me and you'll be safe and sound."

It was time for him to go, but I realized I desperately wanted him to stay. "Would you like a drink?" I offered. "While I get my medicine?"

"Sure." He held his arm out. "Lead the way."

Axel followed me into the kitchen and I found the bottle with the strong pain relievers. I'd only taken them a few times, wary of the risk of addiction. That was the last thing I needed. Popping one, I turned and realized he already had a glass of water held out.

"Thanks," I murmured around the pill, then swallowed it down. The pain intensified then, so I had to set it down and put my fingers on my temples. "It's getting worse."

"Come on. Let me help you upstairs."

I didn't strictly *need* help up the stairs, but the thought of being alone in the house made my head pound harder. "Thank you."

He put an arm around me, and his touch calmed me. I'd never been into aura reading, but something about Axel and his family had a certain presence about them that put me at ease. Especially Axel.

All the way up the stairs, he had one arm around my shoulders and the other on my bicep.

I didn't feel trapped. I felt cherished. Taken care of.

Fuck, I wasn't about to refuse that. I needed it.

Axel wasn't my type, but that didn't mean he couldn't be my friend. And he was already a better friend than any I'd ever had, besides Ava, of course.

I kicked off my shoes into my closet and took off my sweater carefully, trying not to wince when it aggravated my ribs. I wore a modest tank under, so nothing provocative or inappropriate. Axel cleared his throat and turned the blankets on my bed back. I slid between them and scooted over.

He sat on the edge. "Can I get you anything?"

I looked down in time to see his fingers twitch, almost like he wanted to brush my hair back, but that would've been too intimate for two people who'd only really known each other a day.

"Would you stay?" I asked.

Damn it. I hadn't meant to ask him to stay. But I hadn't been alone in the house, as far as I knew, since I got there. Ava was careful if she went out that she made sure Maddox or Maverick were there. I didn't know how she knew. I hadn't told her, but I was utterly terrified Logan would show up.

Axel's face softened and he smiled a sad smile. "I'd be honored. Are you worried about being alone?"

I nodded. "I'm so sorry. I'm being such a burden."

He shook his head and adjusted himself, sitting better on the bed with one leg bent. "You're not a burden. You're a friend in need of a little assistance. I might be the one needing your help one day. Would you refuse me?"

Never in a million years. "Of course not."

"See?"

"Talk to me, please." The pain had been steadily intensifying. I needed the pill to kick in, and soon. "Tell me about your childhood."

He chuckled. "There's not much to tell." But he tried anyway. He talked about growing up here, knowing everyone. Small-town life.

His melodic voice lulled me nearly to sleep. I woke up a little when a stray thought crossed my mind.

I could get used to this.

Which meant it could never happen again.

Chapter 5 - Axel

Charlotte's mouth had fallen open when the medicine kicked in. She hadn't snored, but she'd breathed a little heavier. It was time for me to go. I stalled a little longer, telling her how I couldn't wait to care for her. I'd finally allowed myself to brush her hair away from her face, and when I'd felt the silk of her tresses, it nearly undid me.

Asher growled. *Mate.*

His impatience pushed me away from the bed. It wasn't like we could claim her then and there, anyway. For starters, she was unconscious.

I'd gone downstairs and flipped through the channels until Ava came back with the whole family. Maverick drove them down in my patrol car, so I'd have something to drive back. Not that I couldn't have flown, which is what I'd done the moment I got back to the manor. Ava had asked me why I'd stayed once she went to sleep.

"To keep her safe, of course," I'd said. Didn't they realize? "She doesn't like to be alone."

Ava had nodded. "I know."

I hadn't seen her since then. Three days ago.

Maverick walked out of the back door of the manor and sat beside me, holding out a beer. I'd just finished one, so I took it. Beer didn't affect dragon shifters as fast as humans, not by half. "Thanks."

"How are you?" he asked, settling into the rocker. Mom kept the back porch cleared of snow. She didn't spend much time out here this time of year, but my brothers and Dad and I had fire inside us. The snow and cold didn't touch us.

"Fine." That was a damn lie. "I'm struggling. But staying away, taking it slow, that's best for Charlotte." I wanted this to work as fast as it possibly could, and if I rushed it, something would go wrong and I'd have to back off for potentially longer. Going slow was the only option.

Besides, I didn't want to cause her one ounce of pain or confusion. Not the first bit.

"I'm glad you're going slow. It puts Ava's mind at ease, knowing Charlotte will have you, but also that you're going about it the way you are."

Of course, it's all about Maverick and Ava.

I couldn't help the way my thoughts went. Everything in my life seemed to revolve around Maverick, and it had been no better since he'd found his mate and son.

Maverick puffed out a small breath. I glanced at him and realized he looked hurt. Shit, had I projected that thought? I hadn't meant to.

"Is that really how you feel?" Maverick asked in a soft voice.

Damn it. I sighed and took a long drink. "Not totally." That didn't change the expression on his face.

"Look, Mav. I've had a hard time dealing with being the oldest but not being alpha. You know that. And then we moved. And then we moved back. It's the nature of you being the alpha, and mostly I understand it, truly I do."

"But?" He raised his eyebrows, waiting for more, but didn't seem mad.

"But, part of me resents you. It was bad after we moved back, and I had to leave Jenna." My chest tightened at the thought of the only woman I'd ever loved. "That was a rough time."

That was years ago, though, and I'd moved past it, for the most part.

"I never meant to cast a shadow. Moving to Arizona, you know I wish more than anything I could go back and undo what I did to that kid. Not just because of the mess it caused in his life, but Ava and Maddox. The only good thing that came out of that separation was Hailey."

Ava's daughter was a blessing. Smart as a whip, she already had every one of us wrapped around her finger. I didn't spend as much time with her as the others, not even Jury since he was around Maddox so much. Yet I'd still kill or die for the precocious little girl.

"I know. And moving back was the right thing to do. Hell, I might not have ever met Charlotte. And this situation is difficult, but shit, she's my mate. How cool is that?"

Maverick grinned. "Amazing. So many dragons never find that."

Not even our parents were fated. They were deeply in love, always had been. They were a wonderful match. But this, this pull toward Charlotte, it was a supernatural force I couldn't fight much longer.

But I would. I had to. Whatever it took to make her comfortable and happy.

"It's not you, Mav. I feel helpless. I want to find the man that hurt her, but I won't get that far away from her."

"Let the law have its due process. She's agreed to press charges."

He was right. Besides, if I did find the asshole, I might have a real Maverick moment with him and beat him nearly to death. That wouldn't be a good thing, however badly Asher wanted me to do it.

"I'm just thinking negatively lately. Angry about what happened to her. The pain it caused her and the delays it's causing us."

Maverick drained his beer. "I understand completely. Don't you think I wanted to kill Ava's ex for cheating on her and hurting her and the kids?" He blinked. "Not that it's about me."

Laughing, I shoved at his shoulder. "Don't get all paranoid on me."

"Would you have been happier staying in Arizona?" he asked, his voice serious again.

I stared at him, my little brother. He'd caused me so much irritation over the years. I didn't want to think I was jealous, but I had to admit I'd struggled with it. "A few weeks ago, I'd say yes. I thought about moving back many times."

"But now?" He looked hopeful.

"Now, Charlotte's appearance makes me think this was all for a reason. Some higher power, bigger fate, they knew I'd need to be here for her."

"I always wondered why you came back," he admitted. "At the time, I figured you'd stay with Jenna. I'm sorry, Axel. I'm sorry for my part in this rift between us. I could've done better to not cast such a wide shadow."

Well, damn. That made me feel two inches tall. "It's not your fault. You couldn't help being born alpha. I let it grow and fester and push us apart." We'd never been very close, partly from the age difference, partly because of the alpha stuff. But now, as adults, it was easier to see him as my equal, my peer. And maybe grow a friendship. "I'll try to do better."

"As will I." He smiled and leaned forward. "Brother, I came over here because Ava sent me to invite you to dinner. And I wanted to check on you, but mainly dinner."

My ears perked at that. "At your place?"

He nodded with his eyebrows raised. "Mmm-hmmm."

"With Charlotte?"

"No, we figured we'd let her go eat in town by herself while you came over." He gave me a deadpan expression, but it broke fast as he burst into laughter.

"You asshole. Of course, I want to come to eat dinner there." I stood and took our empty bottles into the kitchen. "When?"

"No time like the present." Maverick walked out of the kitchen.

"Okay," I called as I headed for the back stairs. "I'll change and be down."

I didn't wait to hear his reply. When I got to my bedroom, I threw open my closet door and stared at my clothes like they were a complicated geometry problem.

But they were. If I dressed too nicely, it would look obvious. But I wanted to look as good as possible. There wasn't much to do with my face, it was what it was. My hair just needed a quick comb, but what to wear?

After a quick debate with Asher, who was no help whatsoever—he wanted me to let him go in my stead, yeah, right—I ended up with jeans, black boots, and a black and gray flannel button-down shirt. Not fancy, but I didn't look like a schlub either.

Driving was faster, so I hopped in my cruiser and headed down. Before I knew it, I stood outside Ava and

Maverick's front door with my fist poised to knock. Nerves assaulted me, so I sucked in a deep breath. "This is good. This is progress," I whispered, then knocked.

"Come in!" a voice called from deep in the house. Maddox's, I was pretty sure.

The unlocked door opened easily, and the sound of soft laughter reached my ears. It wasn't Ava's.

Charlotte.

Mate.

I moved toward the kitchen, toward the sound of her voice. It sent thrills through me, every lilt and note that came from her mouth. If I was a cartoon, I would've floated in on the music notes that led straight to my mate.

When I stepped into the kitchen, Charlotte stood behind the table, half bent over, putting forks beside plates. She straightened and met my eyes. "Oh," she whispered. Her mouth gaped for a second as her eyes roamed over me. Maverick walked up behind me, waiting in the hallway for me to go farther into the kitchen, but he could damn well wait.

Excellent. I'd picked the right clothes. I knew they fit well and showed off my body. I worked hard on that body, why not be proud of it?

Under her gaze, I wanted to beat my chest and crow. She liked what she saw. "Hello," she said, then averted her eyes back to the table. "Handsome bastard." She whispered it so quietly, a human wouldn't have heard, especially over the sound of the water running in the sink where Ava filled a pot. I was pretty sure Ava hadn't even heard.

I wasn't a human, though, and I heard her loud and clear. Maverick burst into laughter behind me. Yep, he'd heard her, too.

"It's good to see you again, Charlotte." I moved into the room and to the side so Maverick could come in. "How've you been? Any more headaches?"

Her cheeks pinkened as she replied. "No, not since the one you helped me with. I wanted to thank you for that. I felt so bad about imposing, but you helped me out." She didn't meet my eyes.

Oh, she thought I was hot, all right. But she was probably confused about being attracted to me so soon after what she went through. She had no idea that the bond would do that. It would heal her heart, too, if she let it. But telling her too soon might have an adverse effect, so best to keep on the current course.

"It was my pleasure." I moved a little closer to her, fighting the urge to sweep her into my arms. "Anything for a friend." Or my mate.

Her gaze darted up to meet mine for a second, then she stumbled over her words. "Friends. That's nice. Uh, please, sit."

I had no idea where I should sit. Their kitchen table was round and only set for four. "Where are the kids?"

Ava set a large dish on the table with a smooth smile. "I've had such a craving for duck, and neither of them like it. I knew it was a favorite of both yours and Charlotte's, so I asked Carla to feed the kids tonight so we could enjoy each other's company."

Charlotte gave her a suspicious look but didn't comment. "You like duck?" she asked me instead.

I didn't remember ever expressing a preference, but at that moment it was my favorite dish in the entire world. "I'm a fan." I smiled at her and put all the emotion I could into my grin.

"Sit," Maverick boomed. "I'm starved."

We were halfway through dinner, talking about bits of nothing, but damn, it was nice. The last time I felt like this was back in Arizona with Jenna.

The thought of my former flame normally put a strong pang of regret and pain through me, but this time, the feeling had lessened. I didn't ache with pain, though I did regret how everything went down. At the end of the day, Jenna couldn't just leave her life there or her family. That didn't make her a bad person. I wished her well and lots of happiness in life.

Maybe now I'd see myself to some happiness of my own.

After what I went through with Jenna, I wasn't willing, or capable, of giving my heart to anyone who didn't want it. I'd make sure Charlotte was totally on board before I did that. Like I had any choice.

Chapter 6 - Charlotte

Dinner was a true test of my will. Axel sat across from me, directly in my line of sight, of course. He was the most beautiful man I'd ever seen. Ruggedly handsome. If he was a little bulkier, they'd want him for the covers of romance novels.

His flannel shirt fit like a dream, showing off his arms and wide shoulders. He'd rolled up the sleeves before digging into the duck, which, for the record, he obviously *didn't* love. He picked at it.

And it wasn't prepared badly. Ava did a fantastic job on the bird. It was one of the best I'd ever had, with some sort of orange glaze. Was it just an excuse for him to come to dinner? Ava wouldn't try setting me up with anyone so soon after Logan. That couldn't be it. Maybe he wasn't a fan of orange flavors.

If I hadn't been going through all the shit I had, I would've gone for it. I pictured myself riding him like a cowgirl and dropped my fork. By the time I put it in the sink and got another, my blush had receded. I had to stop thinking like that.

Nothing stopped me from appreciating the view. And having a new friend. That was allowed after coming out of a relationship. No problems there.

"Charlotte?" Axel asked. "Are you okay?"

I blinked and looked into his eyes, which were pinched with worry. Glancing left and right, I saw Maverick with a similar expression, but Ava had a sly look in her eyes. Damn it. She knew.

"I'm fine, why?"

"Axel asked you a question," Ava said brightly. "He asked if you needed to run any errands."

Errands. Oh. I focused on the voices that had filtered through my ears and my musings about how hot

Axel was. He'd been offering to take me to run them so I wouldn't have to go alone. "I'm off for the next two days," he said. "I'd be happy to take you anywhere you need to go."

I ducked my head. "Thank you. I'm probably okay, but if I think of anything, I'll tell you."

"Are you sure you're okay?" he asked. "You seemed pretty spaced out. Is it your head?"

No way I was going to admit to him that I was spaced out thinking about all the repercussions of starting a relationship with him. "It's normal after a concussion to space out a little. My symptoms are actually pretty good for the severity of my injury. I'm healing well."

Axel took a bite of his salad and looked at me like he couldn't wait to hear the next thing out of my mouth.

"Surely you saw worse at the hospital?" Ava interjected.

I shot her a grateful glance. "I did. Lots of times. I worked in the ER for years before getting a position in the NICU. Concussions were a daily occurrence, and I saw much worse."

"That's right," Axel said. "You're a nurse?"

I nodded. "Yes, and I miss it, as much as that surprises me. When you work long hours like that, you expect to be thrilled if you get to quit."

Axel nodded. "No, I know what you mean."

"You're a deputy?" I asked. Ava and Maverick ate and bounced their gazes between me and Axel. It wasn't like either of them to be so quiet. I wasn't completely convinced they didn't want something to happen between the two of us.

They'd have to wait. If it ever happened, it would be a while. I was going to do this smart.

"I am. And some days, it feels like you said. Exhausting, and by the end of the day, you're ready to quit and never go back. But I think I'd miss it too much."

He knew what I meant. Some jobs were a true calling. For me, nursing was. And for him, protecting.

"As soon as I'm healed up, I want to find a job here as soon as possible. I think the hospital is close enough, and once I get a few paychecks, I can get a place of my own."

Technically, I had the money now to get a place, but as long as Ava wanted me there, I wanted to stay. They had the room, and the best I could tell, they didn't consider me a burden.

Besides, I'd do the same for them in a heartbeat. Hopefully, they'd never go through anything so traumatic, but if they did, I'd be there.

"I can introduce you to the hospital administrator," Axel said. "In this day and age, it's who you know." Then, he seemed to realize what he'd said. "Not that you wouldn't be able to get the job on your own merits, of course. I'm sure you're an amazing nurse."

I made him sweat a little, just arching my eyebrow at him.

Ava butted in, defending me. "She's an amazing nurse. She's had several commendations during her career."

Axel swallowed, the sound audible all the way across the table. I couldn't hold my laughter anymore and let it out. He slumped in relief. "You scared me."

"I'll take all the help I can get," I said. "Jobs nowadays are half who you know, not how good you are." I stuck my nose up in mock self-importance. "It'll just be a big bonus for the hospital that they'll get a damn good nurse out of it."

Everyone laughed at that and the conversation relaxed again.

Axel said something about their jobs, telling Maverick about a schedule change, and I imagined him in his uniform. *Geez. I bet he fills it out perfectly.*

A tingle shot down to places it had no right tingling. My body broke out in a cold sweat as I once again imagined what it would be like to be with Axel. His gaze swung from Maverick to me as if he sensed my arousal, though of course, that was impossible.

Axel insisted on helping with the dishes, and Maverick sent me and Ava into the living room. She had a glass of wine, but I'd had so many medicines recently that didn't mix well with alcohol that I refrained. I'd never been a big drinker, anyway.

"They're a handsome pair, aren't they?" Ava asked.

I knew it. She wanted me to like Axel. "I suppose. But I'm not thinking much about that right now."

"Oh, of course not. We just thought that if you and Axel became friends, he might be a good distraction. Not that you should jump into bed together or anything."

She sounded sincere, but I wasn't so sure of her motives. Hell, if I was her, I'd want her as my sister-in-law. I'd give her a pass, but I wasn't rushing into anything if there even was anything to rush into. For all I knew, he wasn't even attracted to me and was being nice to his brother's fiancée's best friend.

That would be my luck.

We talked about me working at the hospital, Ava reassuring me she wanted me to stay here.

"We set that roasting pan to soak." Axel walked in the room wiping his hands on his jeans, which only drew my attention to the snug material over his crotch. Damn it.

"I'm going to head out," he said. "Charlotte, I hope you have sweet dreams." His eyes had a fire behind them that made me do a double take. It must've been a trick of the light, because when I looked again, they were just brown and warm, inviting. No fire.

Strange.

I walked over to the door to say goodnight and lock up behind him. As he stepped onto the porch, he turned. "If you need a little personal ASMR, don't hesitate to call me."

My arousal spiked again, stronger this time. His voice was capable of making me horny, even if he was doing nothing more than reading the damn phone book.

This was the worst time possible for my body to be aroused by the sexy man. *Damn it, get it together.*

Axel's expression changed. If I didn't know better, I would've sworn he knew exactly what he was doing to me. But he couldn't. I'd made no outward signs that I was aroused. I hadn't even shifted on my feet.

He backed up. "Mav has my number if you need anything. Or if you decide you'd like some company to run errands."

That was a tempting offer. More cold-weather clothes were always a good thing. I would've loved to have gone shopping, but I'd drag Ava along for that. No sense in torturing Axel while I looked at leggings and sweaters.

When he walked down the porch steps, I shut and locked the door. "I'm going to bed," I called. Ava was wrapped around Maverick on the couch and waved at me.

"Night," Maverick said. His voice was muffled. I didn't want to think about where his lips were. That would make me think about certain lips being in the same spot on my neck.

After I changed into my pajamas, I slid into bed, my body on fire. All I could think about was the way Ava was wrapped around Maverick on the couch. Except when I pictured it, it was me and Axel, and he whispered dirty things into my ears with that sultry voice of his. Damn.

I couldn't stand it. I reached into my bedside table and took out a small box. A tiny silver bullet rested inside. I slipped the fresh batteries from a compartment at the bottom of the box, and switched them out.

Reaching between my legs under the covers, I pressed the button to make it vibrate, then pressed it two more times to take it to its max setting.

As soon as it touched my clit, I had to fight the urge to cry out.

The little machine took me close to an orgasm and fast. It always had, as powerful as it was. As liquid pooled, slicking my hand and the vibrator, I pictured Axel sliding his dick into me with his hands on my knees, stretching me just enough to catch his head on my G-spot.

Moaning as softly as I could, I used the fantasy and little helper to pull my orgasm out, then continued for one more, this time imagining Axel bringing me to an orgasm with his mouth.

I pinched my clit with my other hand, as if Axel had bitten down with just enough pressure, then pressed the bullet to it again, taking me over the edge for the second time.

Panting, I floated back down and turned off the vibrator, setting it on a tissue beside my bed to clean in the morning. I never put it away until I'd washed it.

Seen too much in the ER to allow that. Yuck.

It was way too soon for me to be this hung up on another man. Enough to fantasize about him while giving myself two orgasms.

Since I couldn't get my body on board with the not-jonesing-over-Axel idea, I'd just have to stay far away from him.

What else could I do? I didn't want to repeat my past mistakes *again*. And jumping straight into another relationship would be classic Charlotte.

It was time for a new Charlotte and a new way of life. No more toxic men. No more fast relationships.

And even though I didn't think he was toxic, still,

no more Axel.

Chapter 7 - Axel

I'd gone home and jacked off, but it wasn't enough. Patrol had proved the biggest test of my will I'd ever had, but even sitting at the station was difficult today. I wanted to run flat-out to Ava's house and sweep Charlotte into my arms.

Her scent lingered in my mind, trapping me in a wave of unending desire. I could've blown my load forty times and it still wouldn't have been enough. Nothing would be enough but her. And even then, I wasn't sure I'd be able to let her go for long.

Getting through the day was torture. The town had been running smoothly, very few calls and the ones we had gotten hadn't required anything of me. I had nothing to do but sit and stew about Charlotte.

The phone rang, so I grabbed it. "Black Claw PD," I said in a bored voice.

"May I speak to Axel Kingston?" a strange voice replied.

"This is he." I lost the bored tone and made myself sound more professional. "How can I help you?"

"This is Detective Stevenson from the Santa Fe Police Department. I have an update about your case."

I'd sent all the paperwork over with my name as the point of contact. "Yes?"

"We picked up Logan McDonnall two days ago. He took a minute to track down. He made bail and was due for court this morning, but he never showed. He's currently in contempt. We're still trying to locate him."

"Son of a bitch." This was horrible news.

The deputy sighed. He knew what it meant to have a domestic violence case disappear as well as I did. "Yeah. I wanted to tell you as soon as we were sure so you could warn the vic. She needs to go underground, if she hasn't already."

That fucker wouldn't get close to her if I had anything to do with it. "Thank you, Detective. I appreciate the heads-up."

The sound of the Santa Fe detective hanging up reverberated in my ear as I called Dad back to the station, explaining the situation. He was on patrol duty at the moment. "I've got to go warn Charlotte right away."

"Of course, go. I'll be back at the station in five." He knew how important Charlotte was to me. Without me telling him, he understood. Mates weren't anything to mess around with, especially fated. Our dragons would revolt if we didn't do it right.

We tried to make sure someone was always by the phones in case of emergency, even if that left nobody patrolling. It wasn't like we were overtaxed by the huge crimewaves in the city, after all.

I turned on the patrol car's lights and went straight to Ava's. Maverick was off work, so they were likely home, and Charlotte didn't like leaving at the moment.

Maverick's cruiser and Ava's SUV were both parked in front of the cabin. I pulled in fast, bouncing around on their rough driveway. Mav needed to have it regraveled.

He met me at the door. His dragon hearing would've meant he heard me coming, of course.

"Dad called," he said. "She's upstairs."

He stepped back so I could walk in. "Ava's in the kitchen."

I went in there. "We have to tell her," I said in way of greeting.

Ava nodded. "Yeah. Okay. You're right." She sighed. "Keeping it from her would only make it worse in the long run."

She walked out of the kitchen. I watched her stop at the bottom of the stairs and call up. "Charlotte? Can you come down here?"

Charlotte's footsteps in her bedroom told me she was coming. Mav and I tracked her progress into the hall upstairs, then down the stairs, both of us looking up.

Ava walked back into the kitchen with Charlotte on her heels. "What's going on?"

She sensed the mood in the room because her brow furrowed. "What is it?" She cocked her head and fixed her gaze on me. "You're in uniform."

I was too worried to appreciate the fact that her eyes drank in every inch of my body in my uniform. I logged it away to appreciate another time.

"I've got bad news." My voice came out low and angry. Mainly because I *was* so damn angry.

Her shoulders sank. "Logan?"

I nodded, and Ava took her hand. "Come sit down."

Ava led her to the table to sit. I took the chair beside her and leaned in close. "They arrested him, but he made bail, then didn't show up for court."

Her shoulders sank more as she hunched in on herself. I would've given the world to take the weight off her shoulders that made her shrink like that. "How long?"

"Since?" I asked. The smell of her fear and anxiety permeated the air. Even that was a beautiful aroma, but it made my dragon tense. He hated seeing her like this. So did I.

"Since he made bail."

I thought back to the specifics of what the detective had said. "I'm not sure, I think two days ago. The detective made it sound like Logan made bail pretty fast after being arrested."

"More than enough time for him to get here," she whispered. Her eyes darted around.

The woman was terrified.

Asher bristled inside me. He didn't like seeing our

mate scared. A dragon's mate had no reason to fear

anything in the world, for he would always keep her safe.

That's how the dragons liked to think, anyway.

"You don't need to be afraid," I whispered. "I

wouldn't let anyone hurt you." I said the words from my

heart, but of course she couldn't have known that. I'd never

meant anything more in my life. I'd rip Logan limb from

limb before I let him lay a finger on her.

Charlotte gazed at me for a few seconds, our eyes

locking on each other and the world passing between us.

Then she blinked and sat up straight. "I have to leave."

Jumping up, she hurried out of the kitchen and

toward the stairs. "Wait," I called, right on her heels.

She ignored me and headed upstairs, still slow on

the steps. She looked a million times better than she had,

with only a trace of a black eye left, but she still had to be

in some pain.

Ava and Maverick followed close behind me, and we crowded in Charlotte's bedroom door as she pulled out suitcases from the closet. Behind that were the boxes she'd brought her stuff in, broken down. "Do you have tape?" she asked. "Packing tape?"

Ava pushed past me. "Now hold on," she said. "You can't just pick up and go off by yourself to parts unknown."

Charlotte sucked in a deep breath and pulled open a drawer, grabbing its contents—which looked very lacy and silky—and threw them in one of the suitcases. "I can and will. He knows I'd never go to my family, but even if I would've, they live in the same city. He could've checked quickly. He knows my only other friend lives in Black Claw, and he knows I visited here. We were dating then, remember?"

Ava nodded. "I know, and you're probably right. But if you run now, you'll be running forever."

What other choice did she have? She felt backed into a corner.

Take her home.

Normally, Asher's ideas were too extreme, but this time… "Stay with me," I blurted, stepping into the room. Ava, Charlotte, and Maverick all looked at me incredulously. "I mean, me, my mom and dad, and Jury."

Ava looked back and forth between me and Charlotte. Maverick closed his mouth and had a sudden interest in the paint around the light switch.

Charlotte still gaped at me. "At your house?"

"Yes. You do need protection, right? And who better to protect you than two cops?" I waved toward Ava and Maverick. "And if he shows up here, they can honestly say you're not here, that you were here, heard he got out, and split. And he won't find you here, or your stuff."

"What if he's already here, watching?" She wrung her hands, dry washing as she rocked from one foot to the other.

"We'll get the boys and carry your stuff through the woods tonight. Nobody knows these woods like we do. He won't see us." I shrugged, desperate for her to think it was a good idea.

Ava nodded. "Yeah. And if he *is* out there watching, he'll see you, which will be Carla in your clothes with one of your wigs on, get in my car. I'll drop her at the bus station where James will be waiting to pick her up out the other door, looking nothing like the person I dropped off."

Ava's face lit up with excitement. "While he's going after them, you'll walk up to the house through the woods!"

Charlotte looked half convinced.

"It's convoluted, but it's not a bad plan," Maverick said. "And it's not like there isn't tons of room at the manor. You could use my old bedroom if you'd like."

I nodded. "Or one of the guest rooms, whatever."

"Why would you offer up your home to a stranger?" she asked me point-blank.

Because you're my mate.

"Because it's the right thing to do. What is my job, if not to protect? Besides, you're family now. Ava is family and you're her family, are you not?"

She nodded, looking more and more convinced. "Okay. Maybe."

Ava jumped in. "I think it's the best possible solution on such short notice."

Charlotte studied Ava's face, then mine again. She sighed and threw more clothes in her suitcase. "Lend me a hand. Wherever I go, I have to take my stuff."

She kept on packing, and Ava sent Maverick for tape.

"Put those books in this suitcase. It's easier to carry them when they're on wheels," Charlotte said, ordering me around with ease.

She's our mate. Who else would be so bossy?

Asher chuckled and the corners of my mouth tried to lift.

Maverick returned with tape, so we set up all her boxes. "How did all this stuff fit in your car?" I asked.

She shrugged. "I'm good at packing." She stopped, staring into space. "What about my car? He'll see it here."

"If we're operating under the assumption that he's already watching the house, then Ava could tell him you left it here, maybe that she bought it from you to help you with money."

Her shoulders relaxed. "Oh, that's a good idea."

"We're assuming he'll speak to any of us or that he's already in the vicinity," Maverick said. "I think we'd *know* if someone was out there."

Charlotte snorted. "These woods are massive. There's no way to know for sure."

"I'm sure we can get you to the manor without anyone seeing," I said. "Trust me on that one."

She paused in the act of trying to get the first suitcase to close. "Okay." Her simple word warmed my heart. She'd agreed to trust me. That made me feel like a million bucks.

She took one of the boxes Mav had taped and began piling toiletries in it. I touched her shoulder. "Please let me keep you safe," I whispered. I sensed Ava and Maverick leaving the room quietly.

Charlotte looked over my shoulder, noticing they were gone. "Are you sure?"

"Positive. Let me help you. It's okay to accept help once in a while, you know?"

She shook her head. "How could you know that's something hard for me? Accepting help?"

I laughed and squeezed her arm where my hand still rested. "Because you've had such a hard time accepting any help."

She let her head duck and laughed with me. "Okay. If you're sure, I would greatly appreciate your help."

Asher crowed inside me, delighted.

It won't be long now! We can claim her.

But we won't be worrying about claiming her until we're both ready. For now, all I wanted was to keep her safe and whole. Protect her.

Cherish her.

Chapter 8 - Charlotte

What did I get myself into? Moving into the big house with the man that keeps distracting me and turning me on at a time I shouldn't even entertain the thought of being attracted to another man.

Worst idea ever.

Except, Logan knew Ava was my only option. The thought that he might've been out there in the woods watching right then made my skin crawl.

I would've never said he'd be the type to do this. Two weeks ago? I would've laughed until my stomach hurt.

But now, with my bruises, the pain, the recovery. Living through what I did… I couldn't put anything past Logan anymore.

"Great." Axel grinned at me; way too pleased I'd said yes. He was looking forward to it. "We'll have fun."

Maybe I was reading too much into it. He was probably eager to help out, and we had become friends of a sort. The attraction was probably all on my side.

After all, how attracted could he have been to a woman covered in bruises? Couldn't be much.

"I'm going to go talk to my mother and make sure we have a room that doesn't need freshening. Some of them have been closed up for a while."

I nodded, watching out of the corner of my eye as he almost reached out and touched my arm. He thought better of it and walked out of my sight.

Ava cleared her throat. I jumped, having totally forgotten that she and Maverick were in the corner of the room, supposedly taping boxes together. I hadn't heard a peep from them.

Whirling around, I glared at my best friend and her husband, who looked back at me with a little guilt on their faces.

"What?" I narrowed my eyes and stalked toward them.

Ava shrugged. "Nothing. I'm pleased you're going to be somewhere safe." She pulled me into a hug. "I worry about you."

When I pulled out of the hug and looked at them again, the guilt and odd grins had disappeared from their faces. Maybe I imagined it.

Ava turned to Maverick. "Mav, honey, go make sure nobody is nearby. Check the, uh, trail cams and stuff."

"You have trail cams?" I asked with surprise. I didn't know that.

"Oh, yeah. You never know what will turn up in the woods," Maverick said. "It's almost as good as having a wolf's nose to find things."

I chuckled at that picture, Maverick out in the woods sniffing around until he found Logan.

Maverick left Ava and me to finish packing. It didn't take too long with both of us. I'd brought a car full of stuff, but still, we worked quickly.

"Char." Ava closed the box she'd just filled with my toiletries and sat on my bed. She studied my face as I stood with the tape gun in my hand, waiting to see what she had to say. "I think going to the manor is the safest choice. But if that makes you uncomfortable in any way, Maverick and Maddox are more than capable of protecting you. We can have Jury stay here with Maddox more, too."

Going to the manor was a little nerve-wracking. I didn't know Maverick and Axel's parents very well and staying in a stranger's home always brought stress. "No. You and Mav just got back together, anyway. A houseguest is something you don't need, even without all my extra baggage. If the manor is safest for everyone, that's where I should be. It's not likely he'll even know to look up there anyway."

Ava nodded. "I hope. It's possible he could see us coming and going from up there, but if we come across him, I'll tell him you heard he made bail and took off. Even if he misses our big dramatic play where we take fake-you to the bus stop, I would be able to tell him what bus you took and all that. We can even go so far as to buy a ticket on your credit card."

"That's a great idea!" I pulled my phone out and brought up the bus company's website. "When are we doing this fake-out?" I asked.

The bed bounced as I plopped down beside my best friend. Ava hummed as she thought. "We're going to get you up to the manor under cover tonight. Let's do it this afternoon, assuming he's already in the vicinity."

"If Maverick doesn't find anything in the woods or on the trail cams, should we wait another day?" I didn't know how to pull off such a convoluted plan.

"Maybe, yeah." She took the phone and scrolled through the departure schedule. "Let's wait until he has more info for us."

My stomach growled as we worked. By the time we finished my packing and stacked the boxes and suitcases in the hall, I was starving.

"Leave them," Ava said. "Let's make dinner."

Neither of us felt like cooking, so we slapped together enough sandwiches to feed all the hungry men that would be in and out of the house soon. Dark wasn't far off, and they'd all be back soon.

Axel was the first to return, slipping in the back door so quietly that I squeaked when I turned around with a fresh pitcher of lemonade to put on the table and discovered him standing behind me.

"You can't do that to me!" I exclaimed. "That's mean."

He laughed and steadied my arms, so the lemonade didn't slosh everywhere. "Sorry. I was trying to get in here without being seen."

Maverick came into the kitchen next, from somewhere inside the house, probably Ava's office beside the living room. "I can't find a hint of anyone being in the woods except for us and Carlos's family. They like to hike near here a lot. Nothing on the *trail cams*." I wondered why he said it like that.

Axel nodded his head, furrowing his brow when his brother mentioned the cameras. "Good. If you couldn't find anything on our cameras, then it's very unlikely he's been in the woods."

"Wouldn't it be easy to fool a camera?" I asked.

The sandwiches caught Maverick's eyes and his face lit up. "Yes, but we have a lot of cameras, and they're very good. Motion sensors, the whole shebang. And they're very well hidden. Is this man particularly adept in the woods?"

Logan was good at a lot of things, but I couldn't recall him ever mentioning anything along the lines of camping. "I think he likes to ski," I said, not sure if that would help us here or not.

Axel shrugged and grimaced. "So, it's possible, but not likely?"

I nodded and took a sandwich. The pimento cheese and ham combo was my favorite.

"That looks good," Axel said, eyeing the food in my hand.

Without thinking, I stuck it toward him. "Try it."

As soon as I did, I felt foolish. He wouldn't want to eat after me. And there were three more sandwiches on the platter just like it.

Ava walked in as Axel took a big bite off of the sandwich in my hand. He'd grabbed my wrist to steady it, and the heat of his fingers sent electricity up my arm straight to my nipples. They hardened like the little pointy traitors they were. Thank goodness for a padded bra.

I took my hand and sandwich back from Axel's grip and bit where he'd just had his lips while staring at Ava and daring her to say something. This was nothing sexy. It was a sandwich between friends. One that he'd dug into without a second thought about my mouth being on it. He'd probably thought of it as a yummy sandwich. Not like me, thinking about our lips being in the same spot.

Fuck.

"Honestly, I think we're safe to put the bags in the SUV and take them up, though maybe Axel should escort you through the woods to be safe." Maverick grabbed a sandwich. "I'm positive there's nobody anywhere nearby."

"Go get the bags and take them up now while you're sure," Ava said. "Then, Axel, sneak back and get Charlotte."

They listened to her, taking their sandwiches with them. The sound of their heavy footfalls on the stairs told us they were doing what she'd suggested. "Do they always obey so quickly?" I asked.

She burst out laughing. "No. Definitely not. I think they're on their best behavior for our guests." She tipped her imaginary hat to me. "We need to keep you around at least until that wears off."

We cleaned up the kitchen as they traipsed in and out with the boxes.

"Be back," Axel called, then the front door slammed.

Ava and I had finished in the kitchen, putting all the rest of the sandwiches in the fridge for anyone hungry and cleaning it all up before they came back. Maverick came in the front door, presumably having driven the SUV back. A few minutes later, Axel came in the back door again.

"How'd you go so fast?" I asked. He wasn't breathing hard in the slightest.

Blinking rapidly, it appeared to take him a few seconds to process my question; it wasn't difficult. "I jogged." He grinned. "Any more sandwiches?" He didn't wait for a reply, he just opened the refrigerator to look. "Oh, excellent. I liked that pimento cheese and ham."

Everyone usually did, once they tried it. Most people only ate their pimento cheese alone. Not me. I knew what was right.

"So, my stuff is there. I sneak up tonight, and sometime tomorrow your mom sneaks down in my clothes and goes to the bus stop?" It was going too smoothly. Something was bound to go wrong.

Axel nodded and looked at Maverick. "Yep."

"Will you check the cameras again before we go in the woods?" I asked Maverick. "Please?" I was nervous about traipsing through the forest after dark, even if Axel would be there with me. "Aren't there wolves and mountain lions?"

To say I wasn't outdoorsy was an understatement. It wasn't that I disliked being out in nature, it was more a lack of opportunity. My parents raised me in the city, and that's where I'd lived my life.

"We make sure to keep this area pretty clear of predators." Axel studied his sandwich. "As long as there's no sign of your ex, we're good to go."

"Shouldn't you have a gun?" I asked. If we did come across something or Logan, it made sense that a police officer would have his gun.

He looked up from his sandwich and winked. "I'm well protected."

Maverick chuckled. "Indeed. Charlotte, try not to worry. We're well equipped for this sort of thing. As a family of police officers, this is our forte. We'll be keeping an eye on things."

His words were a comfort. At least I'd run to a place where they were capable of helping me. "Thanks, Maverick." I walked around the table and gave him a big hug. "You're a great brother."

"Brother?" he asked.

I pulled back and looked up—and up—at my bestie's man. "You're Ava's soon-to-be husband, right? She's pretty much my sister. That means I've finally got the brother I always wanted."

He pulled me close again and squeezed me until I squeaked. I was still a little sore.

"Sorry," he exclaimed. "I always wanted a sister." Everyone laughed, but Axel's tones drew my attention. I imagined how I would've felt right after he hugged me.

Definitely not the same.

"I think it's dark enough," Axel said. "You ready?"

Everything but my purse was already up at the manor. I grabbed my small backpack purse from the corner of the counter. "Ready."

Ava pulled me into her arms. "You're going to be fine."

They'd made sure earlier that all the outdoor lighting was turned off. The motion sensors and all the outdoor electrical outlets were on the same breaker, so Maverick had switched it off. We turned out the kitchen lights and made a production about walking into the living room and settling down to watch a movie. After a few minutes, while I got kind of interested in the romantic comedy, Maverick got up and lowered the shades.

"Now. If anyone is out there that we missed, they'll think we're still in here watching this movie. But I'm confident this is overkill and nobody is there."

I hoped he was right, because no matter their reassurances, going out the back door in the dark made me feel halfway panicked. I put my purse on my back and followed Axel out of the darkened kitchen into the dark backyard. The moon shone down on us, illuminating us as well as any floodlight. He took my hand and we rushed across the backyard into the woods.

The walk to the manor went faster than I expected. Not once did he let go of my hand. The trail was well worn, making it easy to stay quiet and walk soundlessly.

Until we'd been walking for about five minutes. He pulled me further into the woods, off the path.

"Where are we going?" I breathed.

Axel stopped and turned, towering over me. He leaned in and put his mouth close to my ear. "I thought I smelled something," he said. "Stay with me." His hot words washed down my neck, sending fear and desire through my body. Damn it. Now I was panicked and turned on.

I didn't question his words. He couldn't have smelled Logan. He wasn't a bloodhound. He probably heard something, and I misheard him, or he misspoke.

After a while, we broke through on the trail again. Or maybe it was another trail, I couldn't tell.

Whatever the trail, I was glad, because going through the woods had been nerve-wracking. Axel tiptoed over the brush like a deer, while I sounded more like a rhinoceros.

We reached a break in the trees and the house came into sudden view. It was beautiful in the moonlight, all regal and freaking enormous.

Axel moved close again. If he kept that up, I couldn't be held responsible for my actions. "We'll walk around to the back to be safe."

I nodded and followed as he led me by my hand around the perimeter of the woods.

Our walk ended too soon. Even though I was nervous about being out in the woods, too exposed, my guilty pleasure of hanging onto Axel made me want to keep going.

We sprinted across their backyard. They had some sort of weird outhouse by the woods. "What's that?" I asked.

"Just like a shower and changing room."

Why in the world would that be out there? "Do you have a pool?"

He opened the back door. "No, but that's something I want to put in, actually."

The appearance of his mother stopped my train of thought. "Oh, good." She pulled out her phone and typed off a few things before slipping it back in her pocket. "I promised your brother I'd text the moment you came in."

Before we could say a word, she hurried across the kitchen and stuck her head out the door I knew to lead to the foyer. "James! They came in the back."

When she returned, she was all smiles. "He was waiting in the foyer for you."

"Thank you," I murmured, but she waved me off.

"Oh, dear, it's our pleasure. You're family now, after all."

Wow. These people really took Maverick and Ava's engagement to heart. What if it didn't work out? Would I still be family then? Probably not.

But, for now, I appreciated their hospitality more than I could ever express. If that meant they thought of me as family, then so be it. I'd never been close to my family, why not Ava's new one?

"I'll show you to your room," Axel said. He took me on a quick tour of the place first. I'd seen the downstairs already, but not all of it, apparently. Tucked behind the foyer, across from the living room, was a formal dining room. "We never use it," he said. "We tease mom that she's waiting for the Queen of England. We didn't even use it when we had all the family in town."

He showed me the living room again, which I'd seen when I had dinner with them. "This used to be a library and a family room behind it, but we knocked down the wall." Axel pointed out the beams where the wall used to be, and I couldn't help but admire his arms as they moved through the air.

The last part of the kitchen was a huge pantry, laundry room, utility room combo. It featured dumbwaiters to the bedrooms upstairs and chutes for the laundry. "This was my mom's insistence."

I loved it. "I don't blame her a bit." The dumbwaiters were big enough for a laundry basket. It was genius.

Upstairs was filled with bedrooms. "The top floor is more bedrooms. Jury took them over and Maddox has also sort of half moved in." Axel pointed to the stairs. "If you need Jury for something, that's the stairs up there, but I can't be responsible for the teenage guy smell."

Laughing, I followed him through a bedroom door. Instantly, I knew it was his. It was relatively neat, with his police belt on a desk that looked unused. The rumpled bed drew my eye, but after that, I stoically refused to look at it again. "This is my room," he said needlessly.

I backtracked out of the room into the hall as he moved my way, clearly not intending for me to stay in there long.

Fine by me. The longer I was in the room, the more I wanted to smell his pillows.

Geez. I needed a chill pill.

"Your room is right across the hall. It used to be Maverick's and it's bigger than the other rooms on this floor. There's a larger option upstairs, but you'd have to dig out Jury's old sports equipment and video games."

Laughing, I opened the door. "I'm sure this will do."

The room was perfect. It might have been Maverick's, but it sure didn't look like it. The walls were light gray with the same dark brown trim as the rest of the house. Bright teal curtains hung over the closed windows. Shades were pulled down, probably a good idea to keep me concealed in the house. "You have your own bathroom through there."

I ran my fingers across the plush bedspread as I walked across the room to peer into the bathroom. The bedspread felt new and the room smelled like fresh linen. Carla had washed everything that day, I bet.

When I turned to face Axel, I noticed all my boxes lined up on the wall beside the door. He grinned. "Will this do?"

Laughing, I jumped onto the bed and lay back with my arms spread. "This is bigger than my first two apartments and smells a thousand times better."

He grinned and walked into the room, by the sound of his boots on the hardwood. I sat up and looked down, realizing the gorgeous wood was protected from the furniture by a large area rug that matched the curtains and bedspread, dark brown with grays and flecks of teal. The colors were perfect for a man or woman, gender neutral. "I'm going to love it here." I spotted a huge shower in the bathroom and smiled. "Yep."

"Give me your phone." Axel held out his hand. I held it out without question. I already trusted him more than most of my own family.

The phone in his pocket rang a few seconds after he typed into mine. "There. Now you have my number. I promised Carlos I'd help him with a domestic dispute tonight. Both parties are supposed to be in the same place at the same time so we can serve a court subpoena." He gave me a sorry look. "I hate to leave."

"Go," I exclaimed. "I'll be fine. I can go settle in with your mom." And offer to help around the house. If I was going to be a burden, I'd do all I could to alleviate it.

"Okay. I'll be back in a bit. Shouldn't take too long." He smiled at me and stepped forward as if to press a kiss to my cheek or hug me or something.

Then he whirled, thinking better of it.

I could've gone for a cheek kiss. Or more. Axel seemed genuine, but after what I'd been through, how could I know? It was too soon to be thinking all these things, damn it!

I waited a few minutes for him to get out of the house, then walked into the hall. My curiosity wouldn't be sated, so I walked to the end of the hall where two more doors stood open. Exploring for a second on my own, I discovered one of them had to be James and Carla's bedroom. I didn't go in there.

The room behind the second door was generic. Not as big as the one I'd been given; it was meant to be a standard guest room. I peeked into the bathroom and found a standard bathtub and shower combo.

They had given me the nice room. Excellent. I didn't want to be a burden, but I couldn't help but feel a little excited about the nice digs.

Making my way downstairs on the plush carpet, I met Carla in the foyer. "Hello, dear," she said. "I was coming up to ask you if you'd like to have some cake."

Nodding, I smiled at her. "Always."

Her face lit up at my answer. "My kind of woman. Come on."

When we got to the kitchen, I found Axel standing with a bowl, eating some sort of concoction with tomato sauce. "Oh, hello," I murmured.

"Hey. Mom delayed me with her hamburger in a bowl. You have to try some."

He held out his spoon in a déjà vu moment of my sandwich earlier.

Feeling bold, I walked across the kitchen, stopping a few feet shy of the spoon and opening my mouth.

The corners of Axel's lips twitched, and he arched one eyebrow as he stepped forward and put the spoon in my mouth.

Cheeseburger flavors exploded, complete with pickle, mustard, lettuce, and tomato. "Oh, my gosh." I whirled around to look at Carla, who beamed. "That's delicious!"

"Thank you, dear. When you raise three starving boys, you find ways to make delicious meals that aren't fattening."

"How is that not fattening?" I asked. Turning toward Axel, I opened up again, like a bird waiting on a worm.

He chuckled and gave me another spoonful.

"No carbs. The only carbs are what's in the tomatoes."

I moaned and rubbed my belly, suddenly ravenous. Axel handed me his empty bowl. "There you go, fill that back up and enjoy."

As soon as he walked out the back door, I turned to the stove, where the dish rested in an enormous electric skillet. "My gosh, how much did you make?" I asked.

Carla laughed again and took the bowl, filling it up. I was glad she did. I would've felt awkward helping myself barely a half-hour after walking through the door for the first time. "We have a lot of people that like to raid my fridge. I usually make large batches of anything I cook."

Carla made me feel at home in no time. The woman was a gem. Soon we were discussing nursing over cake. "I worked on four-east for sixteen years, until we moved away. When we came back, I was a little older and found I preferred to stay home and take care of my boys. Now they're all grown and making families of their own. If I don't get some more grandbabies to keep me busy soon, I might go back to the hospital."

By the time we finished our coffee, and I said something about going to bed, she'd promised she'd call her old boss at the hospital and put in a good word. I wasn't sure how long I'd be in Black Claw, but it seemed as good a place as any to settle down.

I sure as fuck wasn't going back to Santa Fe.

Chapter 9 - Axel

The domestic dispute took half the night. By the time I got home, it was way too late to see Charlotte again. I went to bed frustrated. Knowing my mate was two doors away was far more difficult than I'd imagined it would be.

Before she was under my roof, I'd thought having her close would settle me. Knowing she was safe. Being close by if she needed me.

I felt like a diabetic locked in a room with a cake they couldn't eat.

After tossing and turning all night, I dragged myself out of bed. It was my day off, but I'd made an appointment at the auto mechanic shop to take my truck. It had been making an odd noise. I didn't drive it often—most of my driving was in my cruiser—but if I needed my truck, it had to be working, so off to the shop I went.

Maverick, Dad, and I had to talk long and hard about the baby Alpha, Stefan, that had helped Roman kidnap Ava and tried to kill Maverick. In the end, we'd decided to give him a chance. He'd never had a clan. He needed guidance and redemption, not harsh punishment.

Things had worked out as well as could be expected. Maverick worked out with Stefan a few times a week and he'd helped him get a job at the auto body shop.

"Hello, Axel," Stefan said when I stepped out of my truck. "Good to see you."

I smiled at the boy. He was just a few months older than Jury. "You too, Stefan. How is the new job going?"

His face lit up. "Great!" He'd rented the apartment over the garage on a trial basis. "Todd says I can stay on full-time and he let me sign a year's lease on the apartment."

Todd owned the shop. He was human, but as good a man as they made. "That's wonderful, Stefan."

He held out his hand. "Give me your keys. I'll have you out of here in no time."

He drove the truck around to the garage while I ambled into the shop waiting room. Once he checked it out and let me know how long it would take, I'd either walk over to the police station and catch a ride home or call someone to come get me. I had all day.

Todd walked through the waiting room after a few minutes. "Axel! How's Stefan treating you? Getting the truck fixed?"

I stood and offered him my hand. "He's checking it out now. Everything been going good with him?"

After shaking my hand firmly, Todd sat on the sofa I'd been on. "If I'd known hiring a twenty-two-year-old to do most of the hard work would be so nice, I would've done it years ago."

Laughing, I joined him on the couch to pass the time. "Is he making life easier on you?"

"He's the hardest working kid his age I've ever met. I thought all this generation wanted to laze around and collect a paycheck." The older man shook his head ruefully, but then perked up. "He's great. Thanks for the recommendation. I thought I was taking a risk and doing you and your brother a favor at first, but it turns out it was you folks that did me one." He clapped my knee and got to his feet with a groan. "You yell if you need anything, Axel."

It was nice to hear Stefan was doing so well. A little stability, a fair and honest alpha to guide him and he'd begun to come out of his shell. The few times he'd been up to the house, it was clear he craved family. Belonging. I hoped he continued to thrive here. He'd find his way.

Stefan came out of the bay a few minutes later. "It's this." He held up a part I couldn't even name. A mechanic I was not. After a quick discussion, he assured me it would take only a few hours to fix. I told him I'd be at the station.

"Call me when it's ready and I'll walk back." I could catch up on some paperwork while I waited.

He was right. About three hours later, he walked into the station with my keys.

"Excellent." I took them and followed him outside. "Hop in."

"I can walk back." He stuck his hands in his pockets and smiled.

"Nonsense. It's on my way back home, anyway. Come on."

With a shy duck of his head, he climbed into the passenger seat.

I slammed the truck door and turned it on. It purred like it was brand new, not thirty years old. "You didn't have to come get me. I could use the walk." I patted my stomach, which I worked hard to keep flat and muscular. Even for a dragon, it didn't come naturally. Maverick worked out harder than all of us. As alpha, he had to be in tip-top shape. I couldn't let my little brother show me up.

He scoffed but didn't reply. The drive to the shop took about two minutes, then I turned to him and pulled out my wallet. "What do I owe you?"

Shaking his head, Stefan opened the truck door. "This one's on me. It's the least I can do to thank you and your family for helping me out when I needed it most."

Damn. We'd made the right decision with this kid. Without shutting off the engine, I got out and walked around the truck. "Well, you have to come up to the house for dinner. Sunday?"

He hesitated. "I don't know, I may need to do something." The kid was clearly uncomfortable pushing his newfound life any faster. But he needed a clan. All dragons did.

"Oh, come on. Mom's making ribs and she's the best at them." I waggled my eyebrows. I wasn't exaggerating. My mom was the best cook.

He scuffed his toe and considered. "I do love ribs."

"Good. That settles it. I'll see you at four. Sharp." I left without giving him an opportunity to refuse me. The more he spent time with his kind, the more he'd realize most clans were supportive and helpful to each other. I didn't know his specific background, but it had to have been bad for him to end up in the situation he had with Roman.

I heard the laughter before I got into the house. After parking my truck in our barn that was really more of a large garage, I walked across the front lawn. My advanced hearing picked up the tinkling laughter of women.

What a nice sound to hear. Charlotte's laugh was easily discernible among the others, a huskier sound. Music to my ears. Instead of walking around the house, I cut through.

When I opened the back door, I found a gaggle of ladies laughing harder than before.

"Hello." I gave them all a bemused look.

"Axel!" my mother shouted. "My handsome boy. Don't you think he's handsome?"

Ava nodded enthusiastically and Charlotte flushed.

"I don't think he's handsome," Hailey said from behind her tablet. The sounds of a show that would've sent me running from the room trickled out of her earbud. She only had one in, keeping one ear on the conversation at hand.

"What are you all doing out here?" I asked. They had the heat lamps on, but it was still pretty chilly out there in the January snow.

"Vitamin D," Ava said. "It's good for you, and this porch gets plenty."

Oh. I noticed the reason for their silly behavior as Charlotte picked up a half-empty glass of white wine. "You're drinking?"

She shrugged and opened her mouth to reply, but my mom beat her to it. "It's Saturday. We're adults. We rarely do this, so hush." She was right. If my mother drank more than once or twice a year, I would've been shocked.

Charlotte grinned. "I never do this. Ever."

"Yeah, she's not kidding," Ava said. "Her parents—"

"Hush," Charlotte said sharply. Ava ducked her head and put her fingers over her mouth in a cute gesture.

I didn't want her to think I was pushing for information. Though, I would've pulled out my claws to find out what her parents had done that caused her to refuse to drink. "No, it's okay. You ladies have fun. Hailey, you okay?"

She gave me a thumbs-up without moving. "Yep. They're funny."

If this had been a regular occurrence, I would've tried to remove the child from the exposure. But it was good for her to see that things like alcohol could be enjoyed responsibly and with moderation.

Charlotte took another long drink of the wine. "Should you be drinking that with the pain medicine you're on?" I asked. Probably not my business, but what if she just hadn't considered that?

"I'm not on it as of two days ago," she said. "Just anti-inflammatories and they're OTC."

Over the counter. Okay. She knew more than me, being a nurse. Plus, Mom was a nurse, too. There wasn't much I could add.

"Okay, I'll leave you ladies to your fun. If you need help, you know where to find me."

Charlotte set the glass down and stood. She was unsteady on her feet and my arms itched to reach out and help her, but still, didn't want to overstep.

She stumbled forward, right into my face, and looked me in the eye. Desire washed over me, but this time I was sure it wasn't only my desire I felt. She wanted me as much as I wanted her.

She fights it.

As usual when around others, I did my best to ignore Asher, but Charlotte blinked several times. "What? No. You're too damn handsome." She poked me in the chest as she spoke. I didn't mind. She could poke me anywhere and everywhere if she wanted. "No. Not handsome. Gorgeous." Whirling around, she pointed at Ava and Mom. "And what are gorgeous men?"

They looked at her, bewildered.

"Trouble!" she yelled. "Gorgeous men are trouble!" She threw up her arms and spun, facing me again.

Oh, my.

"My next boyfriend will be average. Plain. Not ugly, 'cause I can only go so far, but he won't be gorgeous, that's for sure." Her blonde hair shone under the sunlight as she tossed her head. She shot me a glare. "That means no *you.*"

A deep growl bubbled up my chest, but I managed to keep it in check. As far as I was concerned, there would be no other boyfriend. I would be it for Charlotte, as soon as she'd had time to come to the same conclusions.

Claim her before it's too late.

"Too late for what?" Charlotte squinted at me.

Whoops. In her inebriated state, her mind was more open. As my mate, she'd be predisposed to hear Asher anyway. With the alcohol, she'd heard him loud and clear.

I had been moving at a snail's pace, giving her all the time and space she needed. I'd known she was my mate for nearly two weeks now. Taking it slow was doable but thinking of her with another man was not. The thought of Charlotte in some other man's arms made me crazy. And Asher was worse inside me. If he tried to talk to me again, she would hear.

Behind Charlotte, Ava and mom stared at me pointedly. They recognized that I needed to excuse myself.

"Well, like I said, I will leave you ladies to your fun." I beat tracks inside. If I'd stayed out there another minute, I might have grabbed Charlotte and pulled her into my arms.

The need to shift grew inside me. Heat bubbled up, and a wisp of smoke floated out of my nostrils. With Charlotte in the backyard, shifting was not an option. It was too soon to tell her. The last thing we needed was her running away to destinations unknown where we might not be able to find her again. We were good trackers, especially with Jury, but we did not have advanced surveillance equipment—outside of our police connections, of course.

That had already been proven when Maverick was unable to find Ava. Shifting would have to wait.

Maybe a cold shower would calm me down. I took off my shoes and shirt, standing in my bedroom about to unbutton my jeans when Jury called my name.

He didn't sound panicked, so I walked up the stairs without worrying. "What's up?" He and Maddox sat around the low table in his room.

Holding out his hand, he raised his eyebrows challengingly. "I think I can beat you arm wrestling, and Maddox thinks I'm crazy."

Sighing, I gave them both a flat look. "You're crazy."

Turning to leave, I had to freeze when he spoke again.

"Okay, then, if you're too scared."

I wasn't scared. More like frustrated and antsy. Maybe kicking my kid brother's ass would help.

Asher growled in agreement.

"Fine."

I dropped to my knees and held out my hand, elbow on the table, left hand flat. "Ready?"

Jury and Maddox looked like two cats that ate canaries. "Did you two bet on this or something?"

Maddox shifted uncomfortably. "If we did?"

"Then I'd say the winner owes me a cut for bringing me into it."

They both laughed. "Fine," Jury said.

Maddox put his hands over ours and counted down from three. "Go," he exclaimed, and I pushed.

Jury surprised me. He'd been working out more than I realized. I thought he spent all his time playing video games and working his sniffer, but I had to focus to keep him from beating me in the first few seconds.

Beating Jury took an embarrassingly long time. As his older brother, I should've whipped his ass in seconds.

The kid was growing up faster than I realized.

After a couple of minutes, I managed to inch his arm down until his knuckles touched the table.

I stood and shook out my arms. "You boys call it a tie. I damn near went under."

Jury grinned. "I almost got you. We'll try again soon."

Yeah, right. Next time I wouldn't let him goad me into it.

Leaving the room had become the top priority. As I jogged down the stairs, I figured at least the arm-wrestling match had distracted me from Charlotte enough to keep me from wanting to shift right there. Until I came out of the stairwell and nearly bowled her over.

She pressed herself against the wall, shocked, but quickly recovered as her eyes roamed my chest. I hadn't even thought twice about being shirtless until her eyes landed on me. Suddenly I was stripped to my soul. Her eyes saw every inch of me, no matter the jeans covering my lower half. My dick felt the weight of her gaze and twitched, hardening in seconds.

"Fuck," she muttered and pushed off the wall. "Fucking gorgeous." Her dark expression turned mischievous. She stalked forward, to Asher's delight. He hummed in pleasure, assuming this was it.

I knew better. She'd just declared me off-limits.

"What I wouldn't like to do to you," she whispered. Trailing her finger up the middle of my chest, I froze and stared into her eyes.

My dick was not frozen. It jumped in my jeans, desperate for Charlotte's attention.

"Too bad," she said and turned away, walking into her bedroom with a swish of her hips.

Asher waited until the door was shut to begin ranting, thankfully. I ran into my bedroom, slamming the door behind me as I stalked forward to my bathroom and closed that door. Now there were three doors between us. Maybe she wouldn't hear him losing his mind.

My jeans hit the floor, followed by my boxers, then I turned the water on as cold as it would go. Smoke rose from my nostrils in a steady stream, and I couldn't see it, but I was pretty sure it came out my ears as well.

Throwing myself under the stream of ice-cold water, I shivered, but the smoke didn't stop. Neither did the erection.

Reaching out of the shower, I opened a drawer in the vanity and pulled out a bottle of oil-based lube. I learned long ago to buy oil-based for the shower. Otherwise, the water washed it all away. When we'd moved back to Black Claw, it was do it myself or suffer from blue balls.

DIY for the win.

The lube spread over my cock easily, and I moved my hand over the head, as tight as I could stand it as I stroked. Charlotte's teasing smile and blue eyes tormented me as my hand moved faster and faster. Closing my eyes, I pretended she was in the shower beside me and it was her hand milking my cock.

Just the picture of her in the shower, her perfect body fuzzy in my fantasy, was enough to make my balls tingle. I didn't want to imagine her body in clear detail. The real thing was sure to be better than anything I could've imagined.

In my mind's eye, her blonde hair darkened as the water ran over it, and her lips swelled as I kissed them.

Her hand tightened at my base. She knew I was close.

"I love you," Charlotte whispered in my ear, and her words took me over the edge. I spurted my hot cum into the shower, opening my eyes and leaving the fantasy as the evidence of my desire washed down the drain.

Not much longer. We'd been alone this long, we could handle it a few more weeks while Charlotte worked through her feelings and learned not to fight the attraction. Then once she knew the truth, we could claim her and make her ours.

Forever.

Chapter 10 - Charlotte

The head pounding woke me up. I tried to fight it and sleep as long as possible, but I had to give up and search for headache medicine and a large glass of water. After gulping it down with the cup from the bathroom, I collapsed on the bed again and was sucked into oblivion.

I woke again a while later with the sun streaming through the windows of my borrowed room. This time I felt more human.

After a long time under the strong water pressure of the enormous shower, I put my hair up in a high bun and dressed in comfortable clothes. Leggings, which I once said I'd never wear—until I tried some on and discovered their comfort—and an enormous t-shirt. Thick, woolen socks finished the ensemble. If I'd been in my own home, I would've gone braless, but alas, I was not. The shower more than made up for it, though.

It was late enough in the day I felt fairly confident Axel would be gone. Surely, he had to work sometime. I remembered the night before. I'd drunk enough for a headache, but not enough to forget. He'd come down the stairs without a damn shirt on. His chest.

Oh, geez. His chest. It was wide and sculpted, with just enough hair for me to want to touch, but not too much. When I'd put the tip of my finger in the center, it had taken every inch of my drunken willpower to walk away and into my room.

Thanks to the little bullet and fresh batteries, I'd helped my plight enough to get to sleep.

I walked down the stairs slowly as smells from the kitchen hit me. That quickened my step. I'd slept long enough for my stomach to recover from all the wine.

"Oh, there you are." Carla walked into the foyer from the living room. "Come on. I made soup."

"What time is it?" I still hadn't asked Ava for my phone back and didn't have any other way to keep track.

"After noon. You weren't kidding when you said you couldn't hold wine, were you?"

I groaned and shook my head as we walked into the kitchen, but then stopped short. Carla ran into my back.

Axel sat at the kitchen table with a big bowl of soup in front of him. "What are you doing here?" I asked. After a second of disappointment that he wasn't in his uniform, I eyed his long-sleeved tee. His shoulders strained the material, as did his sculpted arms. Not a bad replacement for his uniform.

Carla shuffled past me and gave me a look. "He lives here, child. Where else should he be?"

She probably thought I was the rudest person she'd ever met. "Of course." I ducked my head. "I thought you'd be at work or something."

"Two days off in a row, a rare occurrence." He dropped his spoon in his bowl and jumped up. "I made you something."

I watched while he turned to the refrigerator. He pulled out one of those shaker bottles that athletes liked to carry around the gym for their protein shakes. "Here. It's my special hangover cure. It'll get you on your feet in no time."

As a nurse, I knew the best thing for a hangover was to rehydrate, but I wouldn't have refused Axel. He was too cute holding the cup out with a big grin on his face.

I took it with nervous hands. Who knew what it would taste like? Men and their concoctions. Ugh.

I flipped open the cap and looked at the grayish liquid. Oh, lovely. It was thick. I tipped it up and waited a couple of torturous seconds for the liquid to hit my lips.

To my complete surprise, it tasted halfway decent. Like pineapples. I sighed as I gulped it down. It wasn't as good as a smoothie, but it filled my belly. Maybe it would help the dragged-down feeling.

"If you're feeling up to it, I'd love to be your tour guide. Show you around the town." He smiled at me as if that was the best idea he'd ever had.

"I'd love to, but should I be leaving the house under the circumstances?" If Logan was out there looking for me or watching Ava's house, I didn't want him to see me driving around. Plus, we still had the plan of the bus on the back burner. We hadn't done it yet because nobody had seen him. Maverick was pretty insistent that he'd know if Logan had been on his property. I didn't see how, not as enormous as the property was, but somehow, I trusted him. And Axel.

"I figured we'd drive around. We can take my truck, I just had it serviced."

Getting out of the house sounded heavenly. "Maybe we don't go into town, too?" I asked. If we could come up with a way to get out, that would've been great. I wasn't much the outdoorsy type, but I also didn't want to be cooped up in the house anymore. I'd recovered at Ava's, then a couple days here. Everyone had been amazing. So nice and welcoming, but I'd go stir-crazy soon.

"Okay. Let me go change." I turned and grinned at Carla, who already had a beaming smile on her face. "What?"

"Nothing, dear, I'm just glad you're recovering." She took the empty shaker bottle from my hand and walked to the sink with a sniff. I watched her back, trying to figure out if she was crying, but she just rinsed out the bottle and put it in the dishwasher.

"Charlotte," Axel said. "Dress warm. If you'd like, there's a short hike to a beautiful waterfall."

I nodded but wasn't sure I wanted to hike. If it was short enough, maybe.

When I walked back down the stairs ten minutes later in jeans and a sweater, my thick coat slung over my arm, he was dressed and ready.

"You look great. We match." He held out his arm with a chuckle. We'd both put on thick brown sweaters. I'd chosen mine because the brown set off my blonde hair. I pushed his compliment away—It was nice but didn't matter. I wasn't trying to date the man, no matter how much my body wanted me to. He was too hot to date.

But his dark hair and dark eyes looked amazing above the dark brown of his sweater. To be fair, I was certain he could've worn a brown paper bag and looked hot. I'd been told the same, but that was beside the point. "Regular twinsies," I joked and sent him a wink. "Ready?"

He nodded. "I pulled the truck right up to the door, but I also checked our security cameras. No activity recently, so we're safe to take off."

"Great." I pulled a baby-blue-colored beanie out of my coat pocket and shoved it on. My hair curled naturally at the bottom, a blessing from the hair gods. With a beanie on, I looked like a snow bunny.

Oversized sunglasses completed my look. "Just in case," I explained.

Axel chuckled and grabbed a green scarf from the coat tree beside the front door. It didn't match at all, but when he wrapped it around my neck, his body entirely too close to mine, I realized it had to be his. His scent enveloped me like a hug from a spice rack.

"There. Now you can pull that up and cover your hair." He fiddled with the ends, but obviously had no clue how to make it work.

I did. I wrapped it around and tucked my hair in the back until we got away from his property. "Ready."

He held the front door open, then the truck door. Damn it. He was so sweet.

But I wasn't falling for that shit again. I'd already done that too many times. Hot and sweet came with baggage. Something major had to be wrong with him. He was probably just another wolf in hot-man's clothing.

We did go through town, but only one trip straight down Main. I sat back and kept my hands near my face to further obstruct any view that would identify me. On the other side of town, he turned and took us onto the back roads. Then he drove for what seemed like hours, stopping at several places like an antique shop set way out of town. "How do they stay in business?" I asked. We'd gone in and found a beautiful box that was perfect to hold my makeup brushes. I bought it and the sweet older lady that owned the place wrapped it carefully for me. She'd patted my hand when she handed me the bag. Everyone I'd met so far in the town was so kind. Nothing like living in Santa Fe, where everyone pretty much ignored everyone else.

"The whole town knows she's out there. She's not rich, but she sells enough to locals and the occasional tourist to make a living. And last I heard she's got a niece that's graduating high school soon. She's supposed to take over the place and start doing online sales."

"Oh, that's nice. She was so sweet." I watched the beautiful scenery pass by. The roads were clear, though of course the surrounding forest and land was covered in snow. "When does it stop snowing?" I asked.

Axel laughed. "It's only just begun. We're a few days from February, and February and March are our snowiest months. April usually warms a little, but then there's almost always another big snow in May. Some years it's June before it clears away."

My mouth dropped. That was a lot of freaking snow. There was already a good five or six feet packed in most places. "How do the roads stay so clear?"

"You'd be surprised how many snowplows we have. The roads have to stay clear to keep tourists up here skiing. Just be thankful we don't live on the western slope, near Aspen and Breckenridge. They get the real snow. Three hundred inches is child's play to them. We rarely get that much."

"Let's not go in that direction." I shivered at the thought. It was beyond cold here already.

"No, I wouldn't want to either. I like the snow, but it's been nice this year. We've had a very warm winter."

I stared at Axel in shock. *This* was a warm winter? If I decided to settle here, I might have to consider finding a winter home elsewhere. Like Florida. Or the equator.

The area was peaceful, though. I was at ease as Axel showed me an out-of-the-way diner, a gas station set way up on a hill, and several places to pull off and enjoy the incredible view.

When he parked in front of a trail sign, I shivered. "I'm not sure how much I want to hike," I admitted. "I'm not completely healed, and it's so cold."

He turned in the truck to face me. I'd long ago taken off the extra layers in the heat of the truck, removing everything but my sweater. "We can bundle you up. The walk is really short and the payoff is amazing."

He looked so eager I couldn't refuse him. "Okay. If it's close." He nodded, so I began piling on the layers again. Hat, scarf, and a pair of gloves Axel handed me. "Nice. Thanks. I forgot gloves." Then I struggled into the big parka.

Axel burst out laughing as I tried to wiggle my way into it in the truck. I didn't want to get out of the cab of the truck without the parka on, then all the cold would seep into my clothes.

With his help, I got the parka on, but my nerves were shot to hell with every small touch of his hand.

I zipped and buttoned the coat, then jumped out of the truck. Stomping my feet, I prepared myself to spend time in the cold. The sound of the water filled the air, even out in the parking area. We walked through enormous snowdrifts to get to the trail. It started low but inclined sharply, where the snow had been cleared but they'd had to leave a path for hikers to get onto the packed-snow path.

The parka held up to the cold, though my jeans didn't. I would've worn thermals under them, but I didn't have any. Something I'd rectify if I stayed.

At least he was right about the length of the walk. We topped a ridge in about four minutes of brisk walking, with the sound of the water growing louder with every step.

Damn. He was right about the view as well. I gasped as the frozen waterfall came into view.

"Whoa."

Axel stopped so close that his arm and hip brushed mine. "Told you."

"This is gorgeous." I walked forward, getting as close as I could to the ridge.

"There's a way down, but it's really hard to get back up." He looked apologetic.

"It's okay. This is enough for such a cold day."

We walked around a bit, looking at the small spray of water washing over the frozen icicles. "Does it freeze solid?" The bottom of the waterfall was a big sheet of ice, with more of the falling water freezing every second. But then more still came.

"It can. It takes a while and even colder temperatures." Axel stood still, and every time I looked his way, his eyes were on me, not the waterfall.

It wasn't creepy. It was sweet. As if he watched me to make sure I was okay and enjoying myself.

A zing of cold inched up my back from my shivering legs. "I'm freezing," I admitted. "As beautiful as this is."

He jumped and held out his arm to motion for me to walk down the trail ahead of him. I moved slowly down the incline on the snow. It had been easier going up, stomping our feet into the snow for traction. It wasn't as easy to stomp going down.

I made it with only one slip, almost at the bottom. I could see the truck through the trees.

That was my mistake. I looked up at the truck instead of where my feet went and had that split second of terror when my foot didn't land where I expected it to. I windmilled my arms and my stomach lurched.

Then Axel wrapped his arms around me, circling my stomach, and I was able to find my footing.

"Thank you," I whispered, the heat of his arms shooting straight through the many layers of clothing.

He didn't immediately let go. "My pleasure," he said huskily, only releasing me when I moved forward.

It was a damn good thing there was snow everywhere. Otherwise, it might've been too tempting to strip naked and do the McNasty right there in the woods. When we made it safely to the truck, I sighed, half in relief and half in disappointment that some porn-movie level incident hadn't happened. We hadn't accidentally had sex in the woods. He didn't trip and his dick just slipped right in. Nothing like that. Damn.

"So, how do you know about all these spots?" I asked as he turned the truck around.

"I grew up here. Maverick and I spent most of our youth exploring. Before we could drive, we were on our bikes. When we got a little older, we had four-wheelers and snowmobiles."

My eyes lit up. "Snowmobiles?" I leaned toward him. "Do you still have them?"

He shot me a sly look as he turned the wheel. "We do. I don't suppose you'd like a trip on one?"

"I've always wanted to ride one," I said. "They look so fun."

He chuckled. "They are. I don't think Maverick has taken Ava out yet, either. But both of you need to make a trip to town and get warmer clothes, made for being out in this kind of cold."

I thought about how cold my legs had gotten on our very short trek to the waterfall. "Agreed."

He launched into a story about him and Maverick getting lost on the snowmobiles. The story was meant to be funny, but he sounded so sad. "Why the long face about such a fond memory?" I asked.

He shrugged. "I guess I'm forlorn that those times had to change."

I wanted to ask why they'd changed and how and when and a million more questions, but I had to remind myself that he wasn't my boyfriend. He was a friend who was helping me out during a hard time.

As I tried to figure out a way to get him to elaborate, he surprised me with a question of his own. "What about your family?"

I cleared my throat. "We're not close," I said. If he didn't have to elaborate, neither did I. No need to explain how my family thought I was a bubble-headed waste of time. Since I hadn't gone into money like they wanted, it had cemented their derision of... well, me.

"I understand. Sometimes family is who you choose, not who you're born to." He said the perfect words to comfort me. I avoided thinking about my family most of the time because inevitably I'd end up mad or upset.

"True."

"Hungry?" The little diner had just come into view up the road. "We could grab a bite before going home."

"Sure," I said. "Sounds good."

The risk of running into Logan seemed low this far away from town. There was no reason he'd look anywhere but Ava's house.

Axel helped me into my coat again. We were only running from the truck to the restaurant, but it was that cold. As soon as I was bundled, I made a dash for the door, but he still beat me there, opening it for me.

The diner was half-full, not busy but not dead, either. All the eyes in the room turned to the door as we came in.

And all the women's eyes glued to Axel. "Seems like you're eye-candy around here," I murmured behind him as he led us toward an empty booth.

He snorted. "Hardly. That's Mav."

After a sweet server took our order and brought coffee and tea, I fixed Axel with a firm stare. The time out with him today had done wonders for my mood. I felt more like myself than I had in weeks. "Why don't you have a girlfriend?"

He seemed perfect. Gorgeous, good job, hot, hard worker, funny, sweet, sexy. He lived at home, but I wouldn't have left a house like that, either. What was the point when he was so comfortable there and still single?

His gaze softened as he considered my question. "I've been waiting for the right person."

Axel's left eyebrow arched ever-so-slightly as he answered.

Did he have the same feelings I did? Was he as distracted by me as I was him?

His gaze was intense enough to make me think maybe.

Not that I wanted him to. It was too soon, too much.

But damn it. I really hoped he meant me.

Chapter 11 - Axel

Working the next few days was torture. Nothing happened. No sight of Logan, not even a domestic or fender bender to distract me. Normally, in the middle of winter, everyone stayed home, and things got quieter than normal. We generally spent the time sprucing up the station. Painting, getting small chores out of the way. Sometimes we did extra training classes or took vacations.

But this week, nothing happened, and I nearly went stir-crazy. I knew my entire family was concentrating their available hours to keeping Charlotte safe and entertained, but when I went home two nights later and found out Jury and Maddox had taken Ava and Charlotte out on the snowmobiles while Maverick and I were at work, I nearly throttled the young idiots. I'd wanted to feel her arms wrapped around my waist, watch her eyes light up when we flew over a drift, warm her up when she got too cold.

Damn kid brother. He was a nuisance.

I walked in the back door after a long, boring shift to a kitchen full of family. I'd forgotten it was family dinner night.

"Hey, get in here," Dad called. "You're late."

"Carlos was running behind," I explained. After I hung my gun belt on the hooks by the back door, I joined them at the table. Tacos were laid out, buffet style. "This looks great, Mom."

Charlotte cleared her throat and gave me a haughty look. "What?"

"Charlotte made dinner," Mom said. "I took the evening off and had a long bath."

"It's great," Maddox said around a mouth full of meat, cheese, and who knew what all ingredients the human vacuum had piled on his taco. "Fanks."

Charlotte laughed and shoved his shoulder. "Don't be rude."

"Well, I'm sure it's delicious." I dug into the bowls and piled ingredients on a softshell.

"Axel, you haven't said hello to our guest," my mother chided.

I looked up in surprise and looked down the long table to find Stefan sitting on the other side of Maddox. "Sorry, man, I totally didn't see you there! This family is so big you just blend in as one of us. You'll have to come more often." I got up and walked around the table to shake his hand. I wanted him to feel at home with us and welcome.

I moved my plate across from Stefan, on the other side of Maverick so I could include him in the conversation, but Maverick had something more private to speak of first. It wasn't a secret, and of course Stefan could hear us, as a dragon himself. But it wasn't something we wanted to blast out and worry Charlotte with.

Maverick leaned in. "Any news?"

I shook my head. "No, not from New Mexico. Anything on the trail cams?" Of course, every time we said trail cameras, what we really meant was us and Carlos's pack patrolling the property. Their noses were better than ours, but still, if a stranger was on our land, we could smell it within a mile. That's why our driveway was so long, to keep the smells of town from confusing our sniffers. I wasn't sure originally how Ava's grandmother had ended up with her acre of land and cottage bordering ours. The Kingston land wrapped around Ava's all the way to the area that belonged to the government and town.

As soon as Ava and Maverick were married it would all be Kingston land since Dad had signed everything over to Mav when he became alpha, but it would probably always feel like Ava's. And Mav would never dream of making her feel like it belonged to anyone but her.

"The longer we go without any news, the more nervous I get." We spoke in hushed tones. I knew the dragons at the table heard us loud and clear, but the humans didn't. I didn't want to risk alarming Charlotte after all she'd been through.

She's been coming out of her shell more and more. I'd hate for anything to make her revert to the terrified state she was in when she arrived.

"I need a little cover," I whispered. "I need to shift."

Maverick nodded. He knew the feeling. There were times we weren't able to shift, and it wasn't usually a big deal. But if we went long enough, we started feeling anxious.

I was beyond anxious. My nerves were shot from fighting boredom and worry while at work and trying not to slam Charlotte's bedroom door open and claim her every night. I wouldn't dream of doing it before she was ready, but the slow pace was driving Asher nuts.

"Axel, do you think you could come down to the cabin tonight and help me with something on my truck?" Maverick asked in a loud voice. Everyone looked at us, but the men knew what we were up to.

"Sure. When?" I took a big bite of taco and hoped he said soon.

"As soon as you're done eating, if you can."

"I can come help," Stefan offered. He probably overheard that we needed to shift.

"Sure," Maverick said. "The more the merrier."

I nodded, casual. Hopefully, Charlotte didn't offer to come down, too.

"Oh, you're going out?" she asked.

I nodded and wished I could wait to go shift, but I had to go. If I waited much longer, Asher would force it. She looked disappointed, which was a knife straight to the gut.

Mom must've realized what we were up to. "Ava, Hailey, Charlotte, let's make cupcakes after dinner."

Ava and Charlotte looked less than enthused, but neither of them were rude enough to refuse my mother anything. Of course, Hailey was instantly excited and began chattering about how to decorate them.

I wasn't upset, myself. It would be nice to go shift, have a good flight, then come home to fresh cupcakes.

As soon as I took my last bite, Maverick stood. "Ready?"

I looked at Charlotte, still taking dainty bites of her dinner. "Have a good night." I wanted to make sure she knew I spoke to her especially.

Her cheeks pinkened. She knew I wasn't addressing the entire room, but mainly only her. Good.

We walked out of the house and into the woods, taking the same path I'd brought Charlotte to the house with. This time we didn't take any random detours. The only reason I'd done that was I caught a faint whiff of a stranger. As soon as we got to the house, I'd texted Mav and Carlos, and they'd checked it out but found nothing. Sometimes stray scents carried in the air from farther away and threw us off. As a tracker, Jury was able to better discern those scents, as were the wolves.

We jogged down the path, sure-footed even on the snow. Stefan kept up like a champ. When we reached the clearing of the cabin's backyard, I stripped, handing my brother my clothes. I knew Mav would take my clothes inside for me, so they'd be clean when I returned. "Keep an eye on her," I said. "I'll hurry as much as Asher will let me." Stefan watched with his mouth open. Maverick would explain.

He nodded and pursed his lips. "Go, brother. I've got your back."

I urged Asher to take a wide circuit up the mountain, deeper into our property while avoiding the manor on the off chance Charlotte stepped outside or looked out the back windows.

Every mile Asher flew away from Charlotte, I encouraged him to turn back. I knew he needed his time to stretch and explore, and usually, I gave him all the time he needed. I loved flying with him. But right now, we were needed most at home.

After about an hour, he grumbled, his voice box rumbling his enormous body. But he turned back. *Thanks, buddy.*

Maverick was gone when we landed in the backyard. Asher allowed me to shift back, and even I was cold being completely naked in the snow. I scampered in the back door and changed, listening. Nobody in the house. They must've all been up at the manor.

It took only minutes to run back. When I went full speed, I could've beaten the best human. Of course, no dragon would ever do that.

Charlotte's face greeted me through the back door as I approached the house. She stood at the sink, in front of the window, probably washing dishes by the movement of what I could see of her body.

The snow on the back porch muffled my footfalls as I peered in the window on the back door. The rest of the kitchen was empty.

As soon as I opened the door, I knew why. I heard a movie going in the other room.

"Hey," Charlotte said. She turned from the sink and dried her hands. "Did you finish changing that belt thing?"

I nodded. Eventually, I'd need to confess I didn't know how to change a belt. Mechanics weren't my strong suit. I could change a tire and oil, but that was about it. "Mav watching the movie?"

She nodded. "I felt restless and excused myself. I figured I could do the dishes, so your mom didn't have to."

Cupcakes covered the island, decorated in bright pinks, greens, and blues. "I see Hailey's been at it."

"I had to have her make another batch," she said, looking down and fiddling with the cakes. "Your brothers and dad and Madd ate them all."

She'd made a second batch. For me? "You didn't have to do that."

Her blue eyes met mine when I said that. "I saw how you licked your lips when your mom mentioned cupcakes. I wanted to make sure you got some."

My breath caught in my throat. She'd thought of me.

Before I second-guessed it, my feet moved me forward, into her space. So close I could reach up and cup her cheek.

So, I did.

Her breathing shallowed as she looked up into my eyes. Then, she licked her lips.

And it was over for me. I lowered my mouth to hers, barely touching her lips with mine. I gave her all the time she needed to pull away or tell me to buzz off.

She stepped closer.

Asher panted inside me, eager for me to deepen the kiss.

So, I did.

And she responded, pressing her body against mine as my lips explored hers.

To my intense delight, her small tongue darted out and traced the seam of my lips.

I met it with mine, teasing it, caressing it.

When my hands itched to move around and pull her harder into me, I pulled back.

This was progress, amazing progress. But I couldn't push it too far too fast. She'd run and that would take even more time to recover from.

One step at a time. "Goodnight," I said, my voice husky. I pressed one more soft kiss to her lips, then made my exit, leaving her panting in the middle of the kitchen.

One step at a time.

Chapter 12 - Charlotte

Ava's car door slammed behind me. "I'm in so much trouble," I wailed. "Ava, what am I going to do?"

After Axel left me high and dry in the kitchen, kissing me senseless then walking away like nothing happened, it took me exactly five seconds to decide I had to have advice. I'd grabbed Ava from the living room and hauled her out the door and into her SUV.

"Turn on the car, it's freezing!" She turned over the ignition, but it had been off for too long. It would take a minute to warm up.

She looked scared as she turned to me. "What's wrong? Is it Logan?" Her voice went high-pitched. "Did he contact you?"

I had to grab her hand to get her to calm down. "No, it's not Logan. It's Axel. I think I like him. *Like* him."

Her jaw dropped and eyes widened. "Oh. *Oh*." She relaxed and gave me a knowing look that made me laugh. "Well, you could do worse. You certainly *have* done worse."

"I know, but it's so fast. My bruises aren't even totally faded from Logan. It's been two weeks, Ava! I promised myself I wouldn't do this, but…" I moaned. "He's amazing. I can't get him off my mind." The heat finally kicked in, so I reached over and cranked it up. "Ava, I don't want to end up with another failed relationship and a pile of regret."

Ava sighed and looked out the front window at the snow. The nights here were lighter than the nights in Santa Fe. The snow reflected everything, so it didn't seem so pitch black out here in the open. "I think Axel is nothing like any of the guys you've ever dated. He could be good for you."

I leaned back and thought about that. She wouldn't say it if she didn't believe it. She was usually the one preaching caution when I tried to slide headfirst into a relationship like this.

"Char, there's no rush, right?"

There wasn't. I had nowhere to go, especially while they hadn't found Logan yet. "No."

"So, take your time, get to know him, and do what your heart tells you to do." She tapped the steering wheel. "Bam. That easy."

She grabbed my hand. "I'm still freezing, even with the heat working. Come on, let's go eat another cupcake."

She turned the SUV off, then we made a run for the house. When we walked into the kitchen, Axel had returned. His gaze found mine the moment I walked in the room. "Oh, geez," Ava muttered. I ignored her. "You could cut the sexual tension with a dull knife." She looked from me to Axel, then whirled around. "I'm going back in here."

That left Axel and me alone. He approached me, his gaze moving from mine to my lips. "I wanted another cupcake. Did you save me some?"

Without looking away from the gorgeous man, I shuffled sideways to the kitchen island and grabbed a cupcake off the plate. "Here you go."

He cupped my hand in one of his, heat spreading across the back of my fingers and up my arm and took the cupcake with the other. Letting go of me, he put one finger in the frosting, scooped up a fingerful, then put it in his mouth.

I thought this was what women were supposed to do to men to get them all hot and bothered, but as he sucked the icing off of his finger, I realized my breaths were coming out pretty damn fast.

The sexual nature of sucking frosting off of his finger sent goosebumps all over my body and made me swell in places that only an orgasm could fix.

I didn't know what possessed me, but I reached up and scooped a blob of icing onto my finger. Sticking it in my mouth, I gave him a moan to match his own when the flavors of the icing exploded on my tongue. I closed my eyes and tilted my head back as I sucked every morsel of flavor off of my finger. When I opened them, Axel's expression had turned from teasingly sexual to outright sensual.

"You're testing my patience." His voice was low, quiet, and hit me at my core, dampening my panties as effectively as if he'd caressed my nipples. "You're looking at me like you want to eat me, not this cupcake," he said.

Again, a line I would've used. Was he reading my mind? "I wouldn't mind taking a big bite out of that muscular chest I saw last night." And now I'd let him know I remembered our encounter in the hall the night before, even if I'd had far too many drinks.

I barely got the words out of my mouth when he was on me. I had no idea where the cupcake ended up, but Axel's hands went around me, yanking my body into his. He claimed my mouth. It wasn't a kiss. It wasn't a caress. His mouth descended on mine and possessed it in a way I'd never experienced.

After this, I never wanted to be kissed any other way, either. Damn.

His tongue danced with my own, tasting, teasing, tantalizing. His soft lips moved on mine, sucking my bottom lip in, then moving against both, then pressing kisses against me. He kissed the corner of my lips, the tops, the sides. If he could've climbed inside my mouth and massaged my gums, he would've.

My knees buckled as I leaned against Axel. If I had my way, he'd never let me go. Logan who? He didn't matter. Nobody mattered but Axel.

"Say the word," he whispered against my lips after several minutes of taking my breath away. "Say it, and I'll devour you." He growled after saying those words. Well, probably more of a hum low in his throat. People didn't just growl.

Devouring me was such an odd way to phrase it, but I found myself dying for him to devour every inch of me. From my ears to my toes, with special concentration on some of the middle parts.

"I'm in no rush, Charlotte." My name dripped off his tongue like melted chocolate.

Fuuuuuuck.

"I'll wait as long as you need to get over what you've been through. But when you're ready, I'm here, and I want you."

His consideration of my emotions and my needs tugged at my heartstrings the way his kiss tugged at my…

libido strings. I grabbed his face and drew him to my mouth again, earning another zinger of a kiss.

Several minutes later, when my lips were raw and throbbing—as if *that* was enough to make me stop—I panted and stepped back a few feet. "As hot as that was, including the things you said, I do need more time. I'm terrified of plunging face-first into another bad relationship."

Axel smiled, and his eyes reflected something I didn't quite pick up. Affection, maybe. Certainly not love. We'd only known each other for a couple of weeks. "I'll be here when you're ready. I'm not going anywhere."

"I'm scared that I feel anything for you this fast after what I went through. I like you, Axel, and it feels too soon."

His smile turned mischievous. "I'll endeavor to make you like me even more, then." He stepped forward and pressed another kiss to my lips, this one more chaste.

Sort of goodbye. Axel grabbed the cupcake he'd somehow managed to put on the island, then stopped as if he'd had another thought. He grabbed one last kiss after giving me a longing look, then went out the door that led to the foyer and stairs.

Holy shit. That was one of the hottest things I'd ever experienced. I'd be making a huge deposit in the spank bank as soon as I got to my room. If I tried to go up right then, I'd walk into his room instead of mine, and that wouldn't do anything to alleviate my fears of moving too fast. Even as my body wanted me to do just that, my heart squeezed in fear.

I didn't need any more failed relationships, especially not as bad as Logan's, but I didn't know how much longer I could fight these feelings.

Somehow, I knew, though, that Axel would never hurt me. Emotionally or physically. My hesitation was entirely my own. I knew it as surely as I knew my own name.

He didn't have a violent bone in his body.

Chapter 13 - Axel

"Come on, Axel. Come have a drink with me."
Carlos slapped his hand down on my desk. "You look like
someone offed your best friend."

Black Claw was as busy as I'd seen it in a while,
making my shift fly by. That was the good news. But now
it was time to go home, and it was still too soon. I didn't
know that I could stay away from Charlotte if I went home
right now.

Which meant a beer with the guys sounded perfect.
Maybe I'd relax a little and it would give me more time to
chill the hell out.

We walked to the Dragon's Breath, the only bar in
Black Claw. It had been named by a great-great—many
generations back—grandmother or aunt or something.
She'd opened the bar, as a human relative of dragons, and
married a human. She ran the bar until she died, then her

son took over. It was still owned by a distant human cousin. I doubted he realized we were related, though. He'd never mentioned it.

"Hey, Zane," I called. He waved as we walked to the corner of the room where Maverick and I had cornered Stefan last year. Felt like so long ago. Carlos and I settled in and were soon joined by several bar regulars, come for a chat.

My mind was preoccupied and I barely heard a word they said. When I walked out of my room this morning in my uniform and ready to go, Charlotte stood in the middle of the hall in a skimpy robe. "I thought I could get downstairs and back without being noticed this early," she'd whispered.

I'd stared at the lavender robe, too shocked to move. My gaze had drifted lower to find her shapely, long legs bare. Oh, shit. I'd wanted to nuzzle my face in the curve of her knee, then work my way up her thigh—damn it. I'd jerked my gaze upward to her face before I lost control.

Asher hummed his pleasure in our view.

"I…" She looked like a deer in headlights, her big blue eyes wide. "You look nice in your uniform."

"You look nice in your robe," I countered in a gravelly voice.

She squeaked and jerked the sides of the thin silk robe together. "Excuse me."

I'd stepped to the side to let her pass and she slammed her bedroom door in my face. I hadn't known whether to laugh or moan. She'd been so cute standing there shocked. But so sexy it hurt. Literally.

"Axel, man, where's your head at?" Carlos snapped his fingers in front of my face to bring me back to the present.

"Sorry. I'm distracted." The server set beers down in front of us, and I took a pull. I didn't want to break. If I didn't figure out how to channel this energy and frustration, a break would happen. Just because I hadn't tackled Charlotte in the hall this morning didn't mean I hadn't thought about it all damn day.

My phone buzzed in my pocket as I took a second sip of my beer. It was the house line. "Yeah?"

"Son," Dad said. "Your mother and I have decided to take an impromptu mini vacation. I'm taking her to warm weather for my two days off. Nothing has happened with that boy we're all looking for, and we've been craving some alone time. But Jury is down at Maddox's for the evening, and I didn't want to leave Charlotte alone, just in case."

He didn't have to tell me twice. "I'll be right there."

I hung up and grinned at the table full of men. "Sorry, boys. Gotta head home."

Carlos sat up in alarm. "Anything wrong?"

"No," I waved him off and took my coat out of the empty booth beside ours were I'd tossed it. "I just need to go home, no big deal. I'll see you at work tomorrow."

He nodded and settled in to finish his drink.

I wasted no time, half jogging back to the station to get my truck. I'd only managed two sips of the beer, so no problems driving.

Mom and Dad already had their car loaded when I pulled close to the back door. They waited in the kitchen. "She fell asleep on the couch watching a movie," Mom whispered. "We've been moving around the house as quietly as we could." She kissed my cheek. "Jury is staying down at Ava and Mav's tonight since it's Friday. He and Maddox are planning some camping trip, I believe."

"Have fun." I clapped Dad on the back as he ushered Mom out the door. I knew exactly what they were doing. They wanted to leave an empty house for me and

Charlotte. But that didn't mean it was the right time. I had to do this right, or it could all go so wrong.

When they drove off around the back of the house, I turned and stared at the door to the living room. Did I have the strength to just wake her up and send her to bed?

I did. I had to.

Claim her.

She was curled under a small throw blanket, her head tucked on her hands. Her long blonde hair spilled out behind her and over the arm of the couch. I couldn't leave her there like that, she'd end up with a crick in her neck.

She didn't wake when I pulled the blanket off. Maybe I could've carried her to bed without waking her, but when I slid my arm under her head and lifted, I caught a piece of her hair. She whimpered until I adjusted, then opened her eyes. I turned and walked toward the stairs, awake or not, now that I had her in my arms, I had no desire to put her down.

"Are you slipping into my dreams again?" Charlotte asked. She shifted and put her free arm around my neck.

I couldn't help but chuckle as she looked up at me dreamily. "You've been dreaming about me?" That was possibly the best news I'd heard all year.

Her face flooded with pink as her eyes sharpened. I began to climb the stairs as she realized she was awake. "No, of course not." She squirmed, but I was in no danger of dropping her. I could've happily carried her if she weighed twice as much. "You can put me down." Her breathless voice indicated she wanted me to do anything *but* put her down.

"Admit it. You've got a huge crush on me." I looked away with my nose in the air, teasing her. "You can barely keep your hands off me."

"Whose hands are on whom right now? Hmmm?" She tickled the back of my neck, making me snap my gaze back to her. "I think you're projecting your crush onto me."

I would not crush you.

Her brow furrowed. Had she heard him that time? She'd been tipsy, or maybe outright drunk, the last time. I flexed my arms a little to draw her attention. "You will admit it eventually," I said. "You want me." When we reached the upstairs hallway, I stopped in front of her bedroom door, but still didn't put her down. "So, tell me, please. How dirty were these dreams?" I'd woken up the night before to a strange noise, almost like a buzzing sound. I hadn't connected the dots then, but now I was sure. She'd been using a vibrator.

She sighed a long, sensuous sound. My dick went from half-hard to fully erect in an instant. Luckily, I held her higher in my arms, so she didn't feel it.

"Wouldn't you like to know." She pouted out her bottom lip and winked at me.

Damn right I would. I burst out laughing at her fake flirting. "You're amazing," I said when the laughter passed.

"I hope you know that." I set her on her feet, giving her the opportunity to flee the conversation if that's what she wanted.

"You don't smile often," she observed, staring at my mouth. "You should."

That sobered me up. "I know."

She opened her bedroom door. "Come talk?"

The temptation was too strong. I wanted to do far more than talk, but there was no way I could stop myself from going in there when she'd invited me. "Sure," I said.

She hopped onto her bed and scooted over. I sat on the edge.

"So, why don't you smile?" Her body language and open, caring expression indicated she was truly interested.

I decided to be truthful, as much as I could. I wanted to spend the rest of my life with this gorgeous, resilient woman. Might as well start now. "Habit, maybe. I used to be more happy-go-lucky. Lighter spirited, I guess."

I laughed as I realized how silly that sounded. "Maverick changed it."

She scooted forward. "How?"

"When he was a teenager, I guess the tail end of puberty hit him hard." Couldn't really say his first shift was the problem. "He got into a lot of trouble. I'd just graduated high school and he was about to."

"What happened?" She looked so concerned.

I said as much as I could. "He beat up a kid."

Her face paled, and I wished I hadn't gone into specifics. "Don't worry. He's a completely different person now. I'd trust you or Ava or Mom with him. Or any man, for that matter. As long as they aren't trying to attack our family, Mav will hold his temper. Like I said, it was more a hormone-imbalance thing."

She relaxed as I spoke. "Is he on meds?"

Time to tiptoe around the truth. I didn't want to lie to her. "Not now. We moved to Arizona where our grandfather helped him learn to control his temper and channel it into productive energy."

She nodded. "Meditation and working with energy can go a long way."

I nodded. So could shifting, but I wasn't admitting that yet. "We stayed in Arizona for years, and I met someone. Jenna."

Charlotte sat back when I said Jenna's name. "Oh?"

"But then the family decided to move back here." I shrugged. "And Jenna didn't want to come."

She looked confused. "Did you love her?"

I nodded. "I did." Not as much as I was growing to love Charlotte, but I didn't see that at the time. I couldn't have known my true mate would show up. It was such a rare thing. "But my family is close. If I had to choose between staying with them or staying with her, and I did have to choose, I chose them."

She reached over and took my hand. "But it changed you."

"It made me sad. I began to smile less then, I think. And it caused a rift between Mav and me. He was the one pushing the move home. He was the one that caused the move to Arizona. I blamed him for all of it."

She squeezed my hand and shifted a little closer. "And now?"

"Now, I think maybe moving back here wasn't such a bad thing." I was sure of it.

"You need to focus on your own happiness, Axel. Your feelings are just as important as anyone else's in your family. Be selfish. Do what makes your heart warm." She smiled and looked in my eyes.

"Be selfish?" I asked.

She nodded.

"Can I be selfish now?" I arched my eyebrow at her, conveying my intent clearly.

Her lips parted as she sucked in a deep breath. "Yes," she whispered.

Her word spurred me into action. I pulled on her hand so she fell into my lap, then wrapped my arms around her and supported her.

My lips touched hers with a spark of electricity that ran through my body and hopefully hers as well. I couldn't stop my hands from rubbing up and down her back and my mouth from exploring hers. I pressed my tongue against the seam of her lips and dove inside, tasting her again. I'd craved the touch of her tongue to mine like a man dying of thirst.

She shifted, getting on her knees and pressing her upper body into mine. She was as eager as I was.

Her silky hair called to me, so I lifted my hand to bury it in her tresses, gripping and pulling her head back to get access to her throat.

Bite.

I hoped she didn't hear him. The last time she had was because she'd been drunk and her mind wide open.

No biting. Not anytime soon. First, I had to explain it all to her and we were weeks or months away from that being possible. Asher'd just have to be content with what we had for now.

She arched into me again, so I risked it. "Selfish," I muttered as I let my hands roam from her back to her front, under her shirt. The skin on her stomach felt like satin under my fingers.

She gasped when my warm hands caressed her side, still moving upward.

I hadn't felt a bra on her back, so when my hands met the bottom of her breasts without any lace or material on them, I moaned.

Cupping each of her perfect globes, I held them in my hands for a second, enjoying their weight. Not enormous, but more than a handful. She was perfect.

She shook back her hair and grabbed the bottom of her shirt, which I belatedly noticed had kittens all over it, as did her pants. Cutesy pajamas.

That explained the lack of bra.

After whipping the shirt over her head, she stared at her breasts in my hands. Under her scrutiny, I ran my thumbs over the tips of her dark pink nipples and watched them harden.

"You're gorgeous," I whispered. I couldn't wait another moment. Leaning forward, I sucked one perfect nipple into my mouth and ran my tongue across the top, then circled the hardened nub as I sucked.

Charlotte dug her fingers into my arms and moaned. "Axel." My name came out of her mouth in a rush of breath and sounds of pleasure. "More, please."

Yes. I couldn't wait to give her more. I laid her back on her bed and when she shifted, I smelled her need.

After that, my mind went into a frenzy, the desire to bring her pleasure all I could focus on.

She shimmied out of her pajama pants when I put my fingers on the waistband. As I pulled and her perfect body came into view, my breathing quickened. Blood pulsed to my groin like a waterfall. It ached to feel her tight pussy squeeze my dick when we joined for the first time.

She crossed her legs, suddenly shy. "I haven't done much maintenance down there," she whispered. "Not since…"

"Shhh." Her mound had a small plump spot just above the split. I lowered my head as I pushed on her knees, so she'd spread them for me. "You're heaven."

She relaxed with my words. I didn't care a bit that she was stubbly in spots. She clearly trimmed her hair regularly and shaved part of it.

I ran my fingers along the plumpest part of her mound, then lower, tracing her lips but not dipping between. Not yet. She relaxed her legs further and her split opened for me to see.

A drop of white cream, evidence of her desire, sat on the opening I wanted to taste the most.

I couldn't help myself. I leaned forward and lapped at it, gathering up the white cream and moaning as her flavor exploded on my tongue.

She gasped when she felt me at her entrance, so I did it again, spreading her lips with my fingers and licking from her entrance to her clit.

Her breathing moved from heavy to an outright pant as I sucked her clit into my mouth and rolled it with my tongue.

Letting my teeth graze it as I released it, I used one hand to keep her spread to me and slipped a finger inside her with the other. The angle was awkward, but I was able to turn it so I could feel her, moving inside until that perfect spot swelled, ready for me to work it into an orgasm.

Her G-spot, filled with blood, caused her to cry out when I put pressure on it. I lifted my head long enough to grin at her. "You like that?"

"Yes," she cried and buried her fingers in my hair.

I moved my fingers faster as I licked, sucking and worshiping her gorgeous pussy until I brought her to a screaming orgasm in my mouth. Her legs clenched around my head as it swept her away. My imagination ran wild as she made the most alluring noises. Her voice rose from a deep moan to a high-pitched squeal. When she began to relax, the muscles of her inner thighs clenched and unclenched around me. I kept my mouth on her clit until I was sure she was finished and her legs fell away from the side of my head.

Pulling back, I yanked off my shirt and stood at the side of the bed so I could kick off my boots and pants.

Charlotte sat up and grabbed my belt, undoing the button and sliding my pants and boxers down in one smooth motion.

My hard dick sprang loose right in her face. I wasn't sure if she liked giving blow jobs, but I didn't want her to feel like she had to. I bent over and kissed her with the taste of her pussy still on my tongue.

She fell backward, spreading her legs. "Condom?" she whispered against my lips. I grabbed my jeans and pulled out the only one I kept in my wallet. It was potentially too old, but it would have to do. It had been a while. I hadn't been with a woman since Jenna.

After sliding it on, I positioned myself over her. "Are you sure?" I wanted nothing more than to push myself inside her as quickly as possible, but she had to have the final say.

Charlotte reached between her legs and wrapped her fingers around my aching cock. My hips flexed of their own volition as she did, and my head slipped inside her gorgeous slit.

Moaning, I let her guide me in until she moved her hand, then I pressed forward. I fit inside like we'd been measured exactly the perfect length for each other.

She cried out when our bodies pressed together and my cock filled her. "Axel!"

I couldn't hold back anymore. Pumping my hips, I fucked her fast, then slow. Then I laid my body close to hers, moving my hips up and down.

What had I done to get so lucky? "I…" I whispered in her ear. I'd nearly told her I loved her. "You feel amazing," I said instead. "Your pussy is the sweetest honeypot."

She moaned and arched her back. "Harder," she replied. "I'm close to another orgasm."

I moved up again and pulled her knees over my arms, bending her in half. Then I increased my speed, hitting her harder and harder as her moans grew more and more frantic.

"I'm coming, Axel," she cried out. As she threw her head back, my hot cum squirted into the condom, her tight pussy milking an enormous load out of me. I wished our first time hadn't been with a layer of rubber between us, but my euphoria at finally possessing her and she possessing me gave me one of the best orgasms I'd ever had. The pleasure spread throughout my body, exploding in a shower of relief, possession, and the feeling of coming home. I grunted, slowing my strokes as my orgasm faded, and my mind returned to me.

When it stopped, I stared down at her and let her legs relax.

Pulling out, I took off the condom and threw it in the small trash can by the bed, then collapsed beside Charlotte.

She watched me move, her perfect breasts heaving as she basked in the calm happiness of the afterglow.

I snagged the blanket from the end of the bed, snuggled up behind my mate, and covered us both.

She turned on her side and burrowed into my body. Asher hummed and settled in, feeling more centered and grounded than I'd ever noticed him being. Her warm body curved into mine like we'd lain this way all our lives.

I pressed a kiss to her soft shoulder, inhaling her fruity scent. "Do you want me to go?"

"No," she replied. "Stay." She pressed closer so our bodies connected from shoulder to hip to toes.

We fell asleep in each other's arms. For the first time since she'd pulled up into our yard, I felt at ease. Content to hold my mate throughout the night as her steady breaths tickled my ear.

Chapter 14 - Charlotte

The next morning, consciousness came slowly with an overwhelming feeling of happiness. When I fully awoke, I realized Axel still had his arm wrapped around me. Damn, but I didn't want to move an inch.

I must've moved or something, because he grunted and stretched, pressing the front of his body into the back of mine. "Morning," he said in a deep, sultry voice. I couldn't help but think about what that mouth had done to me last night.

"Morning," I whispered. Turning my head, I pulled the sheet up and twisted around until I saw him. "Did you sleep well?"

He nodded. "Better than I have in years. I can't remember when." He squeezed me and pressed his lips to the back of my head. "Did you like me being selfish?"

I giggled and nodded my head, enjoying the feeling of being cherished in his arms.

My new phone beeped on my bedside table. Ava gave it to me last night before I fell asleep in the living room. I'd brought it up here and plugged it in. It had a new number and was registered in her name, so Logan didn't stand a chance of contacting me through it. She'd turned on my old phone long enough to get my contacts from it then turned it off again.

I checked it, saw a text from Ava, and put it back down. I didn't need to reply right away. She'd definitely understand.

"What time did that say?" Axel asked.

I hadn't even looked at the time, so I tapped the screen and it lit up. "Nine."

"Shit!" he exclaimed. "I'm supposed to be at work!"

Scrambling off the far side of the bed, he nearly fell. Catching himself, he darted around the bed.

I stared in fascination at his penis. It bounced gloriously around as he hurried. The uniform he'd taken off the night before lay on my floor, but he ignored it, heading for the door.

When he had his hand on the knob, he turned back and smiled at me. "See you later?"

I grinned and nodded. "Yes."

While I heard him banging around in his room, I sat back against my pillows and waited for the guilt and regret to set in. When Axel burst into my bedroom a few minutes later in a crisp uniform, I still hadn't been able to muster any.

He grabbed his shoes, bent over the bed and popped a kiss on my lips, pausing a second. "I know it's doing things backward, but I have to ask. Can I take you on a date? A real date?"

Butterflies erupted in my stomach. How sweet could a man be? He'd gotten the main payoff from me. Most men would've stopped with that.

"I'd love to go on a real date with you." I clenched the sheet and tried not to grin like an idiot.

Axel *did* grin like an idiot. He popped one more kiss on my lips then ran. I heard his footfalls thump down the stairs, and then a few minutes later the dull thud of a door slamming. Only then did I get up and look out the back window. He hopped in his cruiser, hadn't even put on a coat, and turned over the engine. The front window was frosty. After a few seconds, he hopped out with a hand scraper and scraped off just enough to drive. I laughed as he got back in the car. I'd done that many times when I worked the early shift in winter.

When he was out of sight, I grabbed my phone and lay naked on my bed to check Ava's text.

Call me when you get up.

I hit the speed dial with her number immediately. "Hey," I said. My voice sounded like the cat that ate the canary and there was nothing I could do to stop that.

"What did you do?" Ava sounded as excited as I did.

"Well…"

"Spill it!"

I giggled and explained everything that happened the night before, from the time she left after dropping off my phone.

She gasped, exclaimed, and squealed at all the appropriate times. When I was finished regaling her with the tale of our night—minus some of the more detailed portions—I stopped. "Ava. Am I making a huge mistake?"

She sighed. "Only you can decide what's best for you. But I'm thrilled with this news. I can't help it. The thought of you and Axel together gives me goosebumps."

I banged my bare feet against the bed and squealed. "I can't believe this. I'm so excited and happy but at the same time almost frozen in fear of it going wrong."

Ava giggled again. "You always worry and always jump in with both feet. Whatever you decide, I'm here for you no matter what."

I smiled, even though she couldn't see me.

We hung up and I hopped up and showered, taking care and time to trim and shave and make my body as luxurious as it could be. When I got out, I moisturized myself to the point of being slick, so I had to wait for my skin to dry to put clothes on.

Jury knocked on my bedroom door as I put on a little tinted moisturizer and mascara. "Hey, Axel called and asked me to come back so you wouldn't be alone. Maddox and I are going to be upstairs if you need us, okay?"

"Thanks, Jury! Hey, Madd!"

He yelled hey, but his voice was muffled by the sounds of their footfalls on the stairs.

I spent most of the day playing he loves me, he loves me not in my head. I even made a pro-con list. The day dragged on with me no surer if the thrilling feeling that was filling me was wishful thinking or the start of something wonderful.

He was a great guy from a great family. Handsome, steady job, seemed like the full package.

The biggest con was that I'd never had a long-term relationship. What was I doing wrong that I picked guys that always ended up leaving, or cheating, or having some terrible hidden thing about them?

I had a lot to think about. After I made a few eggs for breakfast and cleaned the kitchen, I decided I needed to get out of the house. I headed up the stairs, stopping halfway up before I entered the teen boys' domain. There was no telling if it was gross or not. "You two feel like a trip to town?" I didn't want to go alone. But if I was going on a date with Axel tonight, I wanted my toes and nails to be pretty, and maybe a hair trim.

"Sure!" Maddox called back. "Be right down."

By the time I got my hair up in a ponytail, put on a cap and found my big sunglasses, they were ready to go. My enormous coat completed my incognito look. If I had the hood up and passed Logan on the street, he'd never recognize me.

I'd never given Axel his scarf back, so I used it to wrap around my neck and the lower part of my face. "Ready," I chirped through the scarf.

Both boys laughed at me, all bundled up. "It's not that cold today," Jury said. "Almost forty, a rare treat."

I pulled the scarf down so I could breathe. "That sounds cold. I'll stick to the big coat."

We rode in the truck Maverick had given Maddox. I squished myself in the middle, to further obstruct any view of me. "Can you take me to a nail salon? Is there one in town?"

"Sure. We can drop you. Just stay there and text us when you're done." They drove straight to the salon. I looked around constantly to see if anyone looked familiar or seemed to be watching me too closely. When we pulled into the small parking lot of the nail salon, Jury slid out and held the door open as Maddox idled the truck beside the entrance. I thanked them and headed straight inside with my gray hood pulled all the way up.

Once inside, I sighed in relief, the familiar smells comforting me. Nail salons smelled the same whether in New York or Wyoming.

"Hello!" I opened my eyes to find a chipper girl standing in front of a nail station. Geez, the place was tiny. It looked much bigger from outside. "How can I help?"

She was very young, maybe twenty at best, with long red hair. Cute as a button but didn't look old enough to have a clue what she was doing. Oh, well, beggars couldn't be choosers. She was the only one there. A door to the side opened, revealing a second half to the shop with hairdressing chairs in the other room. That explained why it looked bigger. Half nail salon, half hair salon. A one-stop shop.

"I'd love to get a mani-pedi, please."

She bobbed her head eagerly. "Of course! Come right over." She poured liquid from a bottle into a basin attached to a plush chair. "I always disinfect in front of my customers, so you know we keep the place spick-n-span."

"That's nice. I'm a nurse, so I've actually seen some of the repercussions of using an unsanitary nail salon."

Her eyes widened. "I love stories like that. Please tell me."

I laughed and climbed into the chair, rolling up my pants and settling my feet to the side while she rinsed the basin. She'd turned on the jets, allowing the cleaner to go through them, and filled it up for a rinse. I launched into my favorite story of an infected toenail and what all we did to clean it, while she looked between what she was doing and me with a fascinated look on her face.

Some people loved the gross stories, some hated them. Ava didn't like to hear about pus and broken bones at all. I wondered if Axel did.

When I finished the story, she was done with the cleaning and filled the tub up one more time with water for the pedicure. "You're Charlotte, aren't you?" she asked.

I nodded, wondering why my reputation had preceded me. "Ava has told me so much about you, I feel like we're best friends."

I laughed and held out my hand. She left my feet to soak in the warm bath and started on my hand at a mobile station. I assumed she'd move to the other side of the chair to do the other hand when she finished this one. It was a nice setup and so relaxing. I settled back to talk while she worked.

Nail salons were so relaxing. Most men didn't know what they were missing out on. "I'm Harley," she said.

"Like the bike?" I hadn't heard that name many times in my life.

"Exactly like the bike. My mama and daddy rode." She ducked her head, focusing on my nails. "Are you planning to settle here?"

We talked throughout the manicure then pedicure as if we were long-lost friends, slipping into a friendly back and forth.

"So, have you met Axel?" Harley asked. I must've blushed because she laughed out loud. "You have. Isn't he hot?"

Instantly, I couldn't help but wonder if she had her own designs on him. "He is," I said carefully. "I'm pampering for a date with him tonight."

She paused in the middle of buffing with a delighted expression. "Ohhh, I'm jelly!" I must've looked concerned because she shook her head. "Oh, about the date, not the man. Don't worry about me. I've got a crush, but it isn't a Kingston man."

I pushed her until she finally spilled the beans. "Okay," she said after several minutes of me trying to guess. The problem was that I only knew three men and two teens in Black Claw.

"It's a man named Stefan." She blushed so deeply that it clashed with her hair.

Recognition dawned. "I forgot about Stefan!" I exclaimed. "He was at dinner the other night." I'd only had eyes for Axel. Stefan was handsome, quiet, and polite. He'd left when Maverick and Axel had, to look at Maverick's truck or something.

I had a stroke of genius. "Hey, we should do a girls' night. We could get Ava in on it, maybe Carla." A girls' night sounded perfect.

Her eyes lit up. "I'd love that so much. I've been taking care of my grandmother for so long, and now that I've got steady work here, I don't have to worry so much. I've never done a girls' night in my life."

My jaw dropped. "You are in for a treat. Ava and I know how to do it right."

She giggled and finished my toes. I texted Madd and told him I was ready. By the time she was done, they'd be here.

We finalized our plans, the only thing pending was which night. I started a group text with her and Ava and we promised to all check our schedules. Ava was thrilled with the idea, as I knew she would be.

Of course, my schedule was wide open, but I didn't have to advertise that. I texted Ava privately that I planned to ask Axel to invite Stefan over when we did girls' night so that we could all end up at the manor and throw Stefan and Harley together. Ava loved the idea. I knew she would like that, too.

As soon as we got home, I headed for my bedroom. It didn't take long to put on a bit more makeup to give me a date look. My nails looked amazing and I put curlers in the ends of my hair while I dressed.

Before I made a final decision on what to wear, I texted Axel.

Little black dress or jeans and a nice shirt?

If he didn't understand what I meant, I'd have a lot to teach the man. Hopefully, he was smart enough to know I needed to know what to wear.

His reply came several minutes later.

Sorry for the delay. Had to ask Ava's advice. She said LBD but wear tights and a sweater.

Okay. We were going somewhere that might be a little chilly.

I didn't literally put on a little black dress. Since I needed tights, I put on my thickest black pair and a red dress that cinched at the waist but flared out a bit like a sixties doo-wop dress. It wasn't the most sensual thing I owned, but it looked good with the tights and against my blonde curls.

In the end, I was happy with how I looked. I had a black crop sweater with shiny beadwork that stopped under the armpit. It was really just sleeves, but it provided warmth while being able to still wear the dress, which was sleeveless.

After putting on black pumps and slipping out the curlers, I gave my hair a toss and headed down the stairs.

I'd timed it right; Axel had just walked down. He heard me coming and turned at the bottom of the stairs, giving me one of those princess-walking-down-the-stairs moments.

Pure heaven.

His eyes followed my progression, mouth slightly open, desire flooding his gaze. "You look amazing. It's taking everything in me not to turn around and follow you right back up the stairs," he said.

I laughed and twirled with a flirty kick. "Is the dress okay for where we're going?"

He nodded, and I took in what he wore. Black slacks and a gray button-up shirt that almost looked shiny. His broad chest pushed against the material, showing how muscly he was. I hoped at some point he rolled up the sleeves. I didn't know what it was, but a dress shirt with the sleeves half rolled up was damn hot on a muscular man. "It's perfect."

He held out my coat. I didn't have a thick dress coat with me. I was pretty sure I'd left it at Logan's apartment, which sucked because it was a nice one.

Well, this would have to do. I couldn't go without it. "Once we get to the restaurant, you won't need it," Axel promised.

He had his truck parked right at the front porch, and after holding the door open for me, he held my hand as we walked down the front steps. Then he held open the truck door. I climbed in as he ran around and hopped in, starting the engine.

He had to have taken the time to warm the truck beforehand because heat blasted from the vents right away. I held my hands up and warmed them. I'd forgotten gloves again.

He told me about his day, getting in late and the guys ribbing him. I teased him myself. The conversation flowed like we'd known each other for years, not weeks.

We pulled into a parking lot nearly an hour later, but it felt like only minutes had gone by.

"Hungry?" he asked.

Now he mentioned it, I was famished. "Yep."

He jumped out of the truck and I waited for him to cross and open my door. He obviously loved being a gentleman, and I was happy to let him.

Axel took my hand in his as we walked into the building. It was a nondescript brick place near a cliff in the mountain. There was probably a good view a few feet past the building. I'd ask him if we could look after dinner.

I watched my feet as I walked into the restaurant. There was an odd step in the doorway and they actually had a sign that said 'watch your step'.

When I lifted my eyes, I gasped.

The entire back of the restaurant was glass. The view from any part of the floor was stunning.

"Mr. Kingston, ma'am, right this way," a host in a suit held out his arm. He had menus in the other hand. Axel put his hand at the small of my back and as he led me toward our table, the full view came into sight. The mountain dropped away, the sight of the surrounding mountains covered in trees and snow was breathtaking.

Now I knew why Ava had said to wear tights and a sweater. Even with the restaurant heat on, the cold came through the window. The tables closest to the windows probably stayed somewhat chilly.

Looking back on that night, I couldn't remember what we ate. I couldn't remember what we talked about, except that I was at ease and comfortable all night. I told him about my family, but he accepted me as I was, never judged.

"They were always negative, harsh. They criticized everything I did. As a result, according to Ava, and I'm sure she's right, I've craved attention my entire life."

"It's natural for good people to want to see good in others. You see people that could be negative and treat you badly, but you want to find their good. Find their value. It's an admirable trait."

His words warmed my heart. He did for me what I tried to do to all the men in my life. He wanted to find my good. Find my value.

"I hate that you've had to go through this. You don't deserve for anyone to treat you with anything but dignity and respect." He leaned forward across the table and took my hand. "I can't promise to be perfect. I'll make mistakes. I'll screw up, I'm sure of it. But I can promise to protect your heart. I promise to not cross the line. You know the line. I won't ever make a mistake that bad."

I knew the line. I knew it damn well. Every man I'd ever dated crossed it. Cheating, hitting me. Disappearing without a trace.

"How can I trust it?" I whispered. "It's so hard to trust."

He squeezed my hand. "You don't have to yet. Just give me time and a chance to prove it."

That much, I could do.

Chapter 15 - Axel

Over the next few days, I managed to take Charlotte out every night. We went to every spot I'd ever wanted to take a date around Black Claw. I even bundled her up for another hike, this time with better underclothes so she stayed warm. I took her to another frozen waterfall with a picnic, but even I got cold, so we came home.

The more time we spent time together, I learned more about her and she opened up. Turned out she was a warm, vibrant woman, full of what my grandfather would've called piss and vinegar. Every moment we spent together, she burrowed further into my heart, cementing her place there. I wanted her because she was my mate and the very fibers of my being belonged to her and she to me. But more than that, I wanted her because she was the woman of my dreams.

The days ran together. I ran home from work as quickly as possible to be able to see her faster, then kept her out as late as I dared.

We didn't repeat our performance in her bedroom. It was hard to resist, but now that we'd done it, I wanted to backtrack and do things right.

Friday morning, Charlotte was in the kitchen when I went down for breakfast. She and my mom worked around each other, making pancakes and bacon.

I offered to help. I never wanted either of them to think I expected them to be in the kitchen. I could cook for myself easily enough.

But I had to admit to myself I was relieved when they both said no. I hated to cook.

In a few minutes, Charlotte set a plate in front of me and joined me with her breakfast. Mom disappeared, shockingly.

Everyone in the family had been giving us as much space as they could all week.

"Ava and I are doing girls' night at Ava's house with Harley from the salon," she said. I raised my eyebrows. I hadn't even known that she knew Harley. "Ava and I were hoping you and Stefan would drop by a little later in the evening. Maybe bring some wine and dinner?"

I chuckled with my mouth full. After a big swig of orange juice, I shook my head at Charlotte. "Why are Stefan and I bringing booze and food?"

"Because Harley has a crush on him!" She winked at me. "We might as well get those two crazy kids together."

She was so cute in her excitement to play matchmaker.

"I've been feeling romantic this week." She widened her eyes and fluttered her eyelashes at me. "I can't help it."

Slapping my hand to my heart, I closed my eyes and sighed. "I suppose it's all my fault?"

"Indeed. So, you'll come, right?"

Like I'd refuse her. "Of course I'll come, and I'll do my best to get Stefan to come with me."

After a kiss that made me want to carry her upstairs and spend the day in bed, I headed to the station. The day crept by with my mind on the evening's festivities. At lunch, I stopped by the service station to ask Stefan to go with me.

He was under a car in the bay. "Want to join us for dinner at Maverick's?" I asked by way of greeting.

Stefan rolled out from under the car, squinting up at me. "Sure."

"Sounds good. Pick you up after work. About five."

"Okay," he said, already under the car again.

I didn't have patrol, so I spent most of the day near the station, taking calls and running paperwork. After

Carlos came to replace me, I swung into the grocery store parking lot to get a couple of bottles of wine. Then I picked up Stefan. He lived above the shop and had taken the time to clean up. A bit.

He wore old, ripped jeans and a threadbare t-shirt under a jean jacket.

"Don't dress up on our account," I teased him.

"It's just dinner with you and Maverick, right?" he asked. I didn't respond as I crossed the road into the Chicken Shack.

Equipped with a huge bucket of chicken and several large sides, we made our way to Ava and Maverick's house. My phone rang when we were a few minutes away and I hit the speaker button.

"Axel." Dad sounded worried. "Bad news, son. I just got a call from the Santa Fe PD. They got a hit on Logan's credit card. He was at a gas station outside Trinidad a few hours ago."

I cursed under my breath. "Trinidad is halfway between here and Santa Fe."

"Yeah. I don't know what took him so long, but it seems he's on his way here now." Damn it. Enough time had passed that I'd hoped he'd given up and was just hiding out, not after Charlotte.

"I wonder what changed. What made him surface now?" I sighed. "Let's get some extra patrols set up. Call Carlos and have his pack do some running tonight, all around the town and our property."

"I don't know. Maverick already got the ball rolling on that. I stopped in at the station to pick up my watch. I'd left it on my desk. The call came in while I was here."

Irritation flashed through me. I hadn't even had a chance to get the ball rolling. It was already done.

"Why is Maverick already on it?" I asked. "Charlotte is my mate. I can protect her. I can take care of it."

"Everyone is trying to help, son."

"I know that, but I should be the one doing it."

"Maverick is the alpha. It's his job to keep everyone in the town safe, including you and your mate." Dad's voice was kind, but that wasn't what I wanted to hear.

"She's not Maverick's to protect! She's mine!" My voice lowered into a growl.

"What's gotten into you, son?" Dad sounded surprised and maybe disappointed.

I didn't answer right away. My resentment faded a little, but not enough to let me back down. I was the firstborn. I should've been the damn alpha. "I'll keep Charlotte safe. And I'll tell Maverick the same."

I hung up the phone and threw it down on the seat behind the bucket of chicken. Stefan stared at me with an eyebrow up and his mouth hanging open. I ignored him as we turned onto Ava's driveway.

"I get it," he said. I cut my eyes at him and didn't respond. "The need to feel useful. Powerful. Like you're not doing enough. I was alone for years, and now I constantly have the need to prove myself. But man, you've got nothing to prove. Your family loves you. And Maverick looks up to you."

I shut off the engine and turned to him. "What are you talking about?"

"Maverick looks up to you, regardless of who is the alpha. You should hear how he talks about you."

I didn't know what he meant. "You're nuts."

Stefan shook his head. "Man, you don't see it at all, do you? Maverick considers you his best friend. His closest confidante. You don't return the feelings, but he doesn't realize that. As far as Maverick is concerned, you're the best brother he could have."

He got out of the truck with the food and headed toward the door while I sat there, stunned. I couldn't stay out in the truck forever, though, so I grabbed the bag of wine and followed him.

Charlotte let us in with a cry of delight. "What are you two doing here?" she asked.

"We thought we'd drop by with dinner," I said as if it was all my idea. My emotions rolled inside me, but I hid it. The ladies didn't need to worry, especially not Charlotte. Maverick, Stefan, and I were more than enough to protect them from one human man. If Logan made any moves tonight, he'd regret it.

She pulled me out of my preoccupation by introducing me to Harley. I'd seen her around and met her before, but it was a ruse. "Axel, this is Harley." The redhead ducked her head at me and smiled. "Harley, do you know Stefan?"

I watched the sweet-looking girl look shyly at Stefan. He scuffed his toe on the floor and smiled at her. "We've met. Nice to see you again."

Maverick came in from the study. "Hey, I didn't know we were having a date night." He took the bag of wine out of my hand and offered to pour glasses.

He was comfortable and easy with us. As he laughed about something or another with Harley and Stefan, I realized it had been ages since I'd just hung out with him. It reminded me of all the time we used to spend together as kids. We always had a lot of fun then.

Why couldn't we get back to that?

We played cards and pretended there was nothing going on with Logan. The girls drank a little too much wine and got loud and silly.

Later, after a fun evening, I pulled Charlotte close. "Thank you," I whispered, nodding toward Maverick across the room. She didn't just do this for Stefan and Harley. She did it for me to spend some stress-free time with my brother. I pressed my lips to hers and gave her a deep kiss.

"You're welcome," she whispered.

Then she hiccupped. "I need more wine."

With a snicker, I followed her into the kitchen to get her just that. Anything she wanted.

Chapter 16 - Charlotte

When I closed the door, leaving Axel in the hall, I sighed and clutched my hands to my chest. We'd gone on another date, making it every single night since the family dinner that we'd spent together in some way. Usually a date, but sometimes simply a quiet evening at home, having dinner with his family or watching a movie with Jury and Maddox.

All the time together had convinced me of one thing. I wanted to stay in Black Claw.

And if I'd decided to stay in town, I had to make some changes. I couldn't live indefinitely at the manor, especially if Axel and I planned to have a real relationship. Living with him before the relationship got off the ground had to be a bad idea.

I shot off a text to Ava. I hadn't seen her in days, since our girls' night, which had gone well for Stefan and Harley, I was pretty sure.

You up? Call me if you are.

The phone rang seconds later. "Hey, babe," Ava said in a chipper voice. "I'm just finishing up a rush job for a new client. What's up?"

I plopped on my bed and threw myself against the pillows with a sigh. "Oh, nothing. I just need to discuss my entire future."

She chuckled. "Hang on. Let me get comfortable. I needed a break, anyway." I waited while she rustled over the line. "Okay. Spill."

"I think I want to stay in Black Claw." That was the main problem. What to do now that I'd made that decision encompassed the rest of it.

"I should hope so. I didn't expect you to do anything but stay here. Were you considering going somewhere else?"

My jaw dropped. "You expected me to stay?"

"Duh. You packed up all your stuff and came here. What else were you planning to do?"

I'd never really decided. "Go back. Or somewhere new. I didn't know."

"All right, you're staying. What's the problem?"

"Um, I can't stay here forever. I need a place to live. And a job."

"Didn't Carla say she'd recommend you at the hospital?"

She had. I hated to impose, especially after I'd been living in her house so long for free. "Think it's okay to remind her?"

"Of course! I'm sure she's still up for it. Go ask her right now before you lose your nerve."

I sighed and sat up. "Okay. You're right. Thanks, Ava."

She made a kissy sound and hung up. She was right, of course. What had I been waiting for? We hadn't heard from Logan in all this time. There was no reason for me to think he knew I was here. He either came here and didn't find me, or he wasn't trying to look. We never even had reason to enact our ridiculous bus plan.

Pressing my ear to the door, I listened for anyone in the hall. I wanted to talk to Carla without anyone around making me nervous. Like Axel.

My entire body went on edge when he was around. For one thing, I'd been waiting on him to put the moves on me again and he hadn't. If he didn't soon, I'd be putting them on him. I was a modern woman. No reason I couldn't let the man I desired know what I wanted.

But it was nice to feel wanted by him. And he made me feel that every time he saw me. He just stopped himself from taking it to the next level again.

No sounds came from the hall, so I cracked my door. I kicked off my shoes and padded down the hall silently in my socks.

As predicted, Carla was in the living room, curled up in one of the armchairs with a book. A roaring fire put out a bunch of heat, making the living room a great place to snuggle in.

Ava didn't live here, never had. Yet she knew Carla would be up. Maybe Maverick had told her.

"Hey," I murmured. I didn't want to scare her.

She jumped anyway. "Oh, Charlotte. Are you all right?"

"Yes, I just wanted to talk to you for a minute, if you're not busy?" What a stupid question. Of course she was busy, she was reading. "I'm sorry to interrupt."

She put her book on the coffee table and pointed to the chair next to her. "Sit. I'm never too busy for you, dear."

What a lovely woman. I wished I'd been raised by a mother as caring. "I've decided to settle down in Black Claw."

Carla's face lit up in the firelight. "That's wonderful, dear. Are you ready for me to set up that meeting at the hospital?"

She knew what I needed without me even having to ask. "Thank you. I'd appreciate that very much. I want to get my own place as soon as possible, but I'll need a job."

I still had my savings but hated to deplete it. If things got bad and Logan turned up, I might need it to run.

"You'll stay here as long as you need to. We have the room, and you're a delight to have around. And may I say, I believe Axel is pleased to have you so close as well."

She gave me a conspiratorial wink. "Is there anything else I can do to help?"

I shook my head. "I don't think so. Thank you so much, again."

The rest of the house felt almost cold after leaving the heat of the fire in the living room. To warm back up, I snuggled under my covers and dreamed about a life free of worry. A settled life, with roots. When I fell asleep, I dreamed of white picket fences and two-point-five kids.

Carla had news for me at breakfast the next morning. We'd been playing a game, each of us trying to rise before the other to make breakfast. I forgot to set my alarm the night before, though, so she had an omelet station set up when I went down.

"This looks great," I exclaimed.

"Come on, build your omelet." Jury and James sat at the table eating. "Axel went in to work early. Said he had some research to do. He asked me to let you know he'd see you this afternoon."

I smiled as I piled peppers and onions in the bowl with the egg. He cared enough to make sure and leave word for me.

"I spoke to the head nurse from my old floor," Carla said.

My hair flew behind my shoulders as I swung my head up. "Already?"

She nodded with a big grin. "We go way back. She said you can stop by anytime today and she'll interview you. She's doing an admin day today, catching up on paperwork, so the timing is perfect."

She'd already written down the details and slid the paper across the counter to me. "There you go."

I looked at the sweet woman in awe. "Thank you."

She winked. "Don't mention it."

Deciding what to wear was the hardest part. I had to look professional, but interview blogs said the clothes should be completely forgettable. The interviewer had to notice me, not my clothes.

Most of my street clothes were bright and cheery. Wearing pretty, bold colors made me feel good.

In the end, I wore muted autumn colors. Brown dress pants, a burnt orange sweater, and simple jewelry. Jury drove me down to Ava's, where my car was still parked. He and Maddox had driven it a few times since I'd come to town, just on the back roads a little. They said a car needed to be driven at least occasionally.

They'd moved it behind the house, on the far side of the shed Ava's Nana had built years ago. If Logan drove by the house or even just into the driveway, he wouldn't have seen it. But if he'd gotten out and snooped, it would've been found.

Axel told me last night about Logan using his credit card about halfway between here and Santa Fe. But that had been days ago, and we hadn't seen hide nor hair of him. Maverick swore nothing was on any of the cameras, especially around the houses.

I felt safe enough going straight to the hospital and back. It wasn't far out of town.

"Are you sure you don't want me to drive you?" Jury asked. "I can study in the car while you're inside."

He was a sweet boy. One day he'd make a sweet boyfriend. "Thank you, but I think it's okay. We've gone this long without a single word."

He nodded. "You've got your new phone?"

I took it out of my purse to show him.

"Then be careful."

I leaned over and ruffled his hair, then headed for my car. She wasn't the newest thing, but I liked her. I'd had her a while.

Unfortunately, we were halfway to the hospital before the heat kicked in. I blasted it the rest of the drive and was warm by the time I got there.

The interview went great. The head nurse was friendly and personable and asked questions I had all the right answers to. About my credentials, my experience. She grilled me on policies and seemed pleased when I told her I could only quote policies of my previous hospital.

"Ours differ somewhat, but you will learn them in no time," were her exact words, making me think she intended to hire me.

"We have openings on a couple of floors, and I need to run everything by HR and complete your background check." She handed me a form and had me go to their lab for an immediate drug test.

I wrote down the opioids I'd taken with the prescription numbers. I'd suspected I might have to test today. I hadn't had them in a couple of weeks, but they could still linger sometimes in the system. Better to say so beforehand than make them chase me down for the answers.

By the time I finished all that, my throat felt like the Sahara and my stomach growled. And it had been a while since I'd had greasy, fried hospital food.

Every hospital cafeteria was the same. Burgers, fries, pre-frozen chicken tenders. And I loved it. I'd forced myself to pack my lunch back in Santa Fe, so I didn't buy cafeteria food too often.

Everything went smoothly until I sat down with my large soda and plate of tenders and fries. The back of my neck prickled.

I didn't want to be obvious, so I munched on a fry, then got up for ketchup. As I crossed the back of the busy cafeteria to get a small ramekin of ketchup, I looked around as if I had no worries in the world.

Too many people had their faces obstructed. Too many men with hoods up and baseball caps low. I couldn't tell who they were. Or if they were Logan.

My breaths quickened as I headed back to my table.

My plate had been moved to the side.

"Shit," I muttered and pulled the tray closer again. When I'd gotten up, it was directly in front of my seat.

Yanking my phone from my bag, I dialed Axel's number. "He's here," I whispered as soon as he answered.

"Where are you?" He didn't fool around with pleasantries, for which I was thankful.

"Hospital cafeteria."

"I'm on my way. Do you see the security guard's desk? It's directly down the hall from the main door of the cafeteria."

I looked around, no longer pretending I didn't know he was here somewhere. "I do."

"Can you get to it?"

People milled everywhere. The hospital was busy, being the only one around for fifty miles. "I think so. There are a lot of people here."

"Wait for the hallway to clear, but don't wait too long." The sound of the police car's siren filled the phone. "I'm on my way."

He hung up, probably couldn't hear me over the siren anyway. Before I could do anything on my phone, it rang again from a private number.

This was a new phone and Ava said she'd requested a number that had never been used before. Nobody had this number except the Kingstons. I hadn't even called my family.

"Hello?" I said shakily. I knew in my gut before he spoke that it was him.

"You've got a lot of nerve." Logan's steely voice cut across the line like a knife to my heart.

"How did you get this number?" My hand shook as I held the phone up to my ear. "Why are you doing this?"

"You left and had me arrested. I don't know how easy it will be for us to work past this, Charlotte."

He thought we were going to get through this? "We aren't working past anything," I said through gritted teeth.

"I know where you are. You'll be dropping the charges and coming home with me."

Hard, cold laughter erupted from my mouth. "I'm not going anywhere with you, you psycho," I whispered.

My shaking fingers finally pressed the button to end the call. His voice came through the earpiece while I tried, but I couldn't tell what he said.

I dialed Ava. I needed to talk to someone until Axel got here. If I was on the phone, maybe Logan would hesitate to make contact. He'd said he knew where I was, but not that he was here. If he wasn't here, then who moved the food?

"Hey, what's up, friend?" Ava said.

"I'm at the hospital, had an interview. Logan's here somewhere."

She gasped. "How do you know? Did you tell Axel? Let me find Maverick."

A sob stuck in my throat. "He called me. On this number."

"Okay, let me get Mav."

"No, Axel's on his way. I'm sure he'll tell Mav and James." I explained about the phone call and food moving. "I'm about to make a break for the guard's desk, but I didn't want to do it without being on the phone with someone. Axel had the siren on and hung up. He doesn't even know Logan called."

She was as worried as me and spoke fast. "Oh, yeah, it gets loud inside the car. Okay. Just stand up and walk to the desk. Don't slow down until you get there."

I did just as she said, stood without warning and headed straight out the glass door of the cafeteria. My skin tingled the whole way down the short hall, but I made it to the guard's desk without anyone approaching or touching me.

"May I help you, miss?" The elderly guard smiled at me from his chair. If push came to shove, he'd be no help, but being near someone official made me feel a teeny bit better.

"Would you mind if I waited here for my boyfriend?" I asked.

Ava giggled in my ear. "Sorry, wrong time to laugh, but he's your boyfriend now?"

"Hush," I hissed into the phone.

The guard looked concerned. "Of course not. Are you okay? Do you need assistance?" He stood and put his hand on my arm.

"I think I'll be okay if I can stay right here," I said.

He nodded and sat back down, looking around the lobby.

"Talk to me," I whispered. Ava began rambling about Maddox's graduation while I looked around the lobby. I didn't see any sign of Logan, but my anxiety wouldn't calm.

It took Axel fifteen minutes to get there. I stayed glued to the guard's station with one hand on the counter the entire time. He came running in and pulled me into his arms. "Are you okay?"

"Bye!" Ava called when she heard him. I looked down at my phone to see that she'd hung up.

Axel walked us over to a bench settled near a fountain at the entrance as people streamed past us. "I'm fine. I feel silly, but when my food was moved."

He pulled back and looked at me in alarm. "Your food?"

I explained the feeling of being watched and my plate being moved across the table while I got ketchup. "And he called me." I couldn't stop the tears then.

He growled, and this time I was sure it was a growl. I leaned back to stare at him in shock. "Axel…" When I looked at his face, two whiffs of smoke puffed out of his nose. My jaw dropped in shock, but as fast as they appeared, I blinked, and they were gone. I had to have imagined it. In the weeks I'd known him, I'd never noticed any sign that he was a smoker.

Axel hugged me again. "Come on, baby. Let's get you out of here." He shifted to put his arm around me and escorted me to his car. I clung to him until he opened the front door to let me slide in. "Jury and Madd can come get your car later today."

I nodded, relieved to be with someone that could take care of the situation for me. I didn't have to worry now.

As he walked around the front of the car with one hand on his gun, I processed the fact that he'd called me baby. At least that was hot. I loved being called pet names.

"Axel," I said carefully as he pulled out of the hospital parking lot. "I'm under a lot of strain, but you growled earlier. And I would've sworn I saw smoke come out of your nose."

He looked at me briefly before returning his gaze to the road. "Smoke?" He chuckled. "I've been known to growl when I'm angry, and Logan threatening you makes me angrier than I think I've ever been in my life."

Even with his admission that he'd growled, something that surely was a sign of a violent person, I didn't feel threatened. Axel made me feel safer than I'd ever felt in my entire life.

"I've got to call the Santa Fe police department as soon as we get home," he said. "We need all hands on deck for this. Dad and Maverick are deputizing a few volunteers to patrol the town as well as our properties."

That comforted me. "I just want a shower. I feel gross, like him seeing me tainted me somehow."

He took my hand. "You're not gross. You're exquisite. But I understand what you mean. A shower might help you clear your head."

We didn't say much else on the drive. He walked me into the house, and I pressed a kiss to his cheek. "Go make the calls. I'll be in the shower."

At least Logan couldn't get to me here. I was safe. This house had three large, capable men in it, with Maverick just down the road with Maddox. And if Logan somehow got past all of them, I'd be ready this time. I had a big knife in my bedside table drawer. It had been an old boyfriend's. He'd told me it was illegal to carry a blade that long, but then when we broke up, he'd left it at my place.

I'd kept the damn thing.

I turned the water as hot as it would go in the massive shower. Stripping, I threw my clothes in the corner, then stepped under the scalding spray.

Damn, it felt good. The water splashed off my head and skin as I stretched and let my worries wash away.

Logan knew where I was.

But that was okay. Axel and his family, and the police department were prepared to defend me. And that was their job to do so, as officers.

Didn't men find women all the time that were hiding from them? Didn't they beat them or kill them? Maybe so, but I had zero intentions of being a victim. I wasn't about that life.

What if Axel was asleep and Logan snuck in? If he had a gun or something, I'd have to go with him. My mind started going a little crazy.

What if he shot Carla? Or Hailey? He'd go to Ava's first, surely. They were in danger. If I left now, maybe I could draw him away.

But then what? He'd chase me the rest of my life, or until one of us killed the other? Running wasn't a good option either.

The worries piled on me until I lowered myself to the floor. Tears poured out of my eyes, mixing with the water from the shower and washing away.

I had to leave. Staying here meant Logan hurting my friends. The only people I cared anything about in the world. I had to run, or the only option would be going back with Logan.

No. I wouldn't do that. And I wouldn't run, no matter what. I would be strong. I would fight.

Sobs burst from my chest. My options were bleak. Wouldn't I ever get to be happy? Couldn't I ever choose the right man, the right job, the right life choice?

My mind flooded with worry, anxiety, and self-doubt.

"Charlotte." Axel's voice broke through my anxiety attack. "It's okay." He shut off the water and wrapped a large towel around me. Before I knew what he was doing, he had me up in his arms.

"I'll get you all wet," I said between sobs.

"I don't care." He carried me to my bed and then ran back to the bathroom. When he came back, he had another towel in his hands.

The sweet man helped me get under the covers, then took the second towel and scooted in close to me, toweling my hair off gently. "I'm here," he whispered. "I won't let anyone hurt you ever again."

The tears kept falling. "I'm so sorry. I've put everyone in danger." He shushed me and put the towel over my shoulders. Wrapping his arms around me, he laid us down, cradling me against him.

"I'll protect you with my life," he whispered.

My heart lurched at the thought of him being hurt. I pulled away and rolled over to face him. "Please don't do that. The thought of you dying…"

Axel smiled and brushed the hair from my eyes. "I guess you're falling for me already, huh?"

I rolled my eyes but didn't deny it. As I snuggled into his chest and enjoyed the feeling of protection and safety, I realized he was right.

I was well on my way to love. And there was no way to stop it if I even wanted to.

Chapter 17 - Axel

Compromise was the foundation of all good relationships. At least, that's what my dad always said.

When Charlotte insisted that she wanted to start the job at the hospital, even with the risk of Logan getting to her there, it took everything in me not to scoop her up and fly her to a remote cabin and hide her away.

She said she'd spent too long hiding. He couldn't keep her from having a real life. Eventually, she had to function like a real person.

In some ways, she was right. It had been weeks. And she'd waited another week from the incident at the hospital to start the job.

She'd reasoned that she was never alone at the hospital. She was on a busy floor and would always be with a patient or coworker. Especially at first, as she'd be training.

I didn't feel any better about it.

We'd had one of Carlos's guys deputized, and he patrolled the hospital during Charlotte's shift. I made him promise to spend most of his time on her floor, but there was some regulation that said if we sent officers, they had to be available for the entire hospital. Plus, Charlotte said she didn't need a bodyguard, and that she'd be embarrassed if everyone found out he was just there because she had a psycho ex.

I'd given in begrudgingly, as long as she agreed to text me every two hours. She promised to try her best.

Carlos's guy was texting me every hour. It gave me peace of mind.

Asher had been restless and upset since the moment we dropped Charlotte off for her shift. That had been our other request. That she let me or Jury or one of my family drive her to and from work.

She hadn't liked that, but she finally agreed. It was the best compromise we could come up with until someone got their hands on Logan and put him in jail.

Maverick had insisted I meet him at the diner for lunch. I walked over from the station and waved at the hostess when I walked in and saw Mav already at a table.

I wanted to ask him about the smoke Charlotte had seen anyway.

"How are you holding up?" he asked after I put in my order. "You look like hell."

I felt like hell. "I can't stop worrying. Can't focus. And when I found out he called her, she caught a glimpse of Asher." I didn't elaborate, he knew what I meant.

He raised his eyebrows. "You've got to tell her soon. You're serious about her, aren't you?"

I gave him a sarcastic look. "Were you serious about Ava?"

He held up his hands and chuckled. "I know. It's natural for you to have reacted like that, but if she doesn't know what's going on, she's likely to freak out."

I sighed, and we both paused the conversation when the food was set in front of us. We were speaking in vague terms, but still, better to be safe.

"The more you fall in love with Charlotte, the more anxious Asher will be until you, uh, complete the deal." He meant claimed her. Until I claimed her, Asher was likely to give me more trouble like letting smoke come out of my nostrils.

"How did it go when you showed Ava?" He'd never told me the story of how he'd told her and Maddox.

He burst out laughing. "That's a story not for a public place. But if you love her and you believe she loves you; she'll accept it. What other choice would she have with the truth right in front of her?"

I munched on a fry and considered his words. "When did you get so smart?"

He snorted. "I've always been smart. You just like to ignore it." He didn't sound angry, though. Just teasing.

We talked about other things as we ate, Maddox's graduation, Hailey's upcoming slumber party. Jury's college career. I realized as I took my last few bites that it was so easy to just hang out with Maverick.

"I'm sorry, Mav. I'm sorry I let a rift grow between us."

He looked at me, surprised.

"I shouldn't have let my jealousy and self-doubt cause years of problems. I'm truly sorry."

Maverick smiled and sighed. "I'm relieved to hear that. I've only wanted us to be friends like we were when we were kids." He poked my hand. "I just want you to be happy. I never meant to take your life away."

He hadn't done anything to overshadow me on purpose. I'd find a way to work through it if he did. "Water under the bridge?" I asked.

His grin broadened. "Under the bridge."

Maybe we could move on and be real brothers again.

We parted soon after, Maverick to go home for a while and me back to the station. I'd arranged to get off just in time to go pick Charlotte up from her shift.

I idled the cruiser at the front door, watching for any signs of Logan or another car that might need to pull up to the door to pick up a patient. A few minutes after I stopped, Charlotte jogged out of the building and hopped in. She leaned over and pressed a kiss to my mouth, then smiled. "Hey, you."

Having her at my side again gave me an instant ease I hadn't felt all day. We were meant to be near one another. "You seem happy," I observed as I pulled away.

"I am. I've only worked three shifts, but they've gone so well. I love the nurses on my floor." She beamed at me. "I'm worried about Logan, of course, but if we can get him in jail, I think I'll love this hospital. This job."

Her happiness and ease warmed my heart. Now if only we could get her asshole ex out of the picture, we could start building a life together. "Hungry?"

She nodded eagerly. "Your mom. I swear, she's the sweetest woman I've ever met."

I chuckled. She'd never seen her after she had to clean Jury's bathroom.

"She packed me a lunch. It was delicious, but the way my day went, I ended up grazing from the lunchbox a little at a time. I stayed full enough most of the day that way, but now I'm starving." She tugged on her scrub top under her coat. "But I sweated pretty much all day." The sun visor squeaked from rarely being used as she pulled it down. "Ugh." She smoothed her hair the best she could as I glanced between her and the road.

"You look beautiful. You always do," I said. "But we don't have to go anywhere fancy."

"How about a burger drive-through?" She looked around the cruiser. "Are you allowed to eat in here?"

I chuckled. "Oh, yes. Do your worst. It can't come anywhere close to the worst this car has seen."

Then I had to tell her the story of the woman that I'd picked up a couple of years back, high out of her mind, stark naked, walking down Main Street in the middle of the night.

She'd peed in the backseat of the cruiser. "And that's why they make them out of that material. So you can open the doors and hose them out."

Charlotte wrinkled her nose and looked through the cage into the back seat. "Gross."

"Yeah." I stopped at the speaker to Burger Master. "Burger?"

She giggled and peered at their big menu board. "Double cheeseburger, no onion, large onion rings, large chocolate milkshake."

I repeated her order to the little microphone-speaker combo, then asked them to double it. "I'll have the same."

As we drove around the building, I fished out my wallet to pay. "No onions, but add onion rings?"

She shrugged. "I am who I am."

Damn, I loved her for that.

We parked at a nearby overlook to eat and enjoy the view.

"I have to talk to you about something," she said between sips of milkshake.

My stomach dropped. Those words rarely led to a good conversation.

"I need your help."

That sounded more promising. "Anything."

"It's time for me to move out of your parents' house." She eyed me as she took a bite of her huge burger.

What was it about a gorgeous woman who was unafraid to eat in front of a man? Hot. That's what it was. Hot.

But I didn't want her to move out. "That's not necessary."

She grunted. "No, but I want to. I love your parents, especially your mom. And Jury has been amazing, like the little brother I always wanted."

"Don't you have a little brother?" I asked, confused.

"Yes, but Jury is the little brother I would've preferred to have."

I chuckled as I realized her intent. "Gotcha."

"Besides, haven't you been giving moving out some thought?" she asked.

I didn't look at her. I'd been mulling it over since we moved back, but instead of moving out, I'd been socking away money. We had family money, of course, but I didn't want to use that. I wanted to build my home with the money I'd earned working at the police station. It was a modest income, but without rent to pay, and my parents not willing to let me chip in on food or utilities, it made sense to save it. I'd put away quite a nest egg over the years.

"I've given it some thought."

She smiled. "I don't think we should necessarily jump into moving in together. But it's something I'd like to do in the future. Maybe we could find a small house or apartment for me to rent for a little while. After that, who knows?" She shrugged and studied her onion rings. "Is that something you'd consider?"

She sounded hesitant. I wanted to pull her into my arms and ask her to marry me right then.

But still, way, *way* too soon.

Instead, I got her to talk about what kind of house she'd like to have if she could build it herself. At first, she put me off by saying she didn't have nearly enough money saved up to build a house.

"I know, but I like talking about my dream home," I countered as I finished my milkshake. "I want a place upstairs that I can throw laundry straight into the laundry room."

Her face lit up. "I love that idea. And those newer soft-close drawers."

I nodded and made mental notes of all the things she said. Once she got started, she rattled on about it. It was something she'd given thought to, even if she hadn't realized it.

She was ready to settle down as much as I was.

When we got home, Char said she was worn out. She'd not questioned me about us still being in two different rooms, but she gave me a lingering look before going up the stairs.

I knew the perfect spot on the property to build the house. I still needed to be on our land, near family, for reasons I hadn't explained to my beautiful mate yet. I had to be able to shift, and dragons needed to be near their clan. But I knew a contractor that could get the ball rolling on the house. It was time to put my savings to good use.

He got right back to me with his email address, so I got my rarely used laptop out and sent over everything I remembered her saying about the house, as well as the location. Then I let Mav know that he might smell Chad and his construction crew poking around Poplar Bluff. That was the spot I wanted for my house. It was pretty high up but had the best view on the entire property.

Everything rolled together with ease. Chad would start laying things out and email me back the next day, and

Mav was thrilled at the idea of me building. I had to swear him to secrecy, of course.

The thought of my home with Charlotte put me in the best mood I'd been in since Logan was spotted last week.

I tiptoed across the hall and into Charlotte's room. She was already asleep, her scrubs crumpled on the floor. I smelled her face cream. She'd come in and washed her face before collapsing in the bed.

Her blonde hair still in its ponytail, I stroked a few stray locks away from her cheek.

This beautiful woman came into my life and turned it on its ear, and I couldn't have been happier. I already loved her deeper than I ever would've thought possible.

I couldn't wait to start our life together.

Chapter 18 - Charlotte

Of course, on my first day off from my new job, Axel had to work. I tried not to be too disappointed. I didn't want to be *that* girl. The one that lost all parts of herself with a relationship. Ignoring my friends would be the worst thing, so I texted Ava and Harley to invite them to lunch.

Ava had a parent-teacher conference, but Harley was eager to go.

We met at the diner, pretty much the only place in town to grab a bite.

Harley grinned at me over her soda. "How's Axel?" She wiggled her eyebrows.

I burst out laughing. "Oh, stop. We haven't…" I wiggled my eyebrows back. "Since the one time."

She nearly squealed. "I didn't know about the first time!"

"Shhh." I looked around the diner to see if anyone was paying us any attention as I giggled with her. "We had one night, but he's not tried to repeat the performance since then. I think he's trying to woo me."

Her face softened and she moaned. "Oh, that's so romantic."

Damn if she wasn't right. It was beyond romantic. "It is. But I'm about ready for that repeat performance."

We dissolved in giggles again and waited for our food.

"I've been thinking about asking him if he wants to find a place together," I said. "I mentioned something about it without coming out and asking, and he got me to talk about my dream home. Neither of us landed on any certain side of moving out, whether together or not."

"Do you want to live with him?" Harley asked simply.

I nodded. "I think I do, but I'm terrified of moving too fast. He's great. The best relationship I've ever had, by far. But what if I rush it too much?"

Harley shook her head. "You can't live in fear. If you do, you'll never do anything worth doing."

The young girl was wise above her years. "Tell me, how is Stefan?" I gave her an eyebrow wiggle as she sighed.

"It isn't happening. He doesn't seem interested."

Disappointment filled me, and I wanted to hug my new friend. "I'm sorry. You two looked so cute together. I wanted it to work out."

She twisted her lips. "Yeah, me too. But it wasn't meant to be, I guess." She hesitated, then continued. "And, a couple of weird things happened. I would've sworn I saw smoke coming out of his nose one night, and then his eyes looked red for just a second."

The smoke sounded just like Axel. How weird. "I'm sure it'll work out. That sounds a little crazy."

I changed the subject away from love and talked about the salon. She was the manager of the nail side of the salon, but one day she wanted to manage the whole thing for the owner. "I took business courses online while I took care of my grandmother," Harley said. "Now that she qualifies for in-home care, I have more time to focus on a more strenuous job."

I encouraged her to pursue it. She might as well do the best she could for herself.

Her lunch break ran out, so we parted ways soon after.

When I got back to the manor, I parked my car out back, near the door, and grabbed my purse, but when I looked out over the snowy yard, a dark blob caught my attention. I walked across the packed snow to get a closer look, hoping hard it wasn't a dead animal.

When I got closer, I realized it was a pile of clothes.

A police uniform, actually. I picked up the shirt. The badge was still clipped to it. They were Axel's clothes. What the hell?

A rustling sound from the woods to my left and slightly behind me made me clutch Axel's shirt to me and whirl, crouching defensively. In this part of the world, any sort of wild animal could've come out of those woods.

But what emerged from the trees was beyond anything I could've imagined in a billion years. I tried to rationalize with myself as I stared at the massive creature. It was bigger than any horse or cow I'd ever seen. More on size with an elephant. It had scales, actual scales. Like a dinosaur or lizard.

It looked toward the house and I sucked in a breath as I tried to turn so I could hide in the little building they had out here. But the snow crunched under my feet and the creature swung its massive head toward me.

Its eyes widened, and when it stepped toward me, I screamed. I couldn't easily get to the house, so I barreled into the woods, down the path I knew would lead me to Ava's, stopping only long enough to tug on the door to the building. Locked. As I focused on keeping my footing, Axel's shirt still clutched in my hands, I made myself stop screaming. That would just give the enormous creature a sure location for me.

I should've tried to get around it and get in the house, but I'd been so scared I hadn't thought straight. I just ran.

When the house came into sight through the trees, I screamed Ava's name and kept screaming it. She heard me, and as I launched onto the porch, she opened the door, then held it for me to run into the house. She jumped out of the way just in time.

I shoved her out of the way and slammed the door shut.

"What in the world is wrong?" she cried. "Is it Logan, should we call Axel and Maverick?"

My lungs burned like I'd inhaled smoke. I was in shape, but I hadn't been working out for weeks, and a run that far and fast had me panting like a forty-year smoker. "Big animal," I gasped, aware of how insane it would sound if I said what I really thought it was—A dragon.

"Oh, boy." Ava sat at the kitchen table. "Big animal, huh?"

"Huge. Lizard thing." I couldn't say it.

Ava nodded. "Calm down," she said.

"Ava," I cried. "I'm not joking! It was as big as an elephant, easily. Maybe bigger."

"I know. I believe you. Here." She stood and shoved a bottle of water in my hand. "Sit down and sip that while I call Maverick."

Even though I didn't know how she was keeping herself together so well, I did as she said. Why wasn't she losing her shit alongside me?

But then, the more I calmed down and my breathing slowed, the more ludicrous it seemed that I'd been chased through the woods by a freaking dragon.

But I'd seen what I'd seen. There was no other way to describe it. It was either a dragon or a dinosaur.

Ava spoke in hushed tones as the back door opened and Axel burst in. He was wearing the clothes that had been in a pile in the snow, with the white undershirt and of course minus the shirt still in my hand.

The scent of smoke followed him into the room. "What's going on?" I asked, my voice shrill and panicked. "Why were your clothes on the ground? I didn't know what to think. Did you see the…creature?" I stood and Axel put his arms around me.

"It's okay," he murmured.

"Why do you smell like smoke?" I cried.

This shit was too damn much.

Ava sighed. "You have to tell her."

Axel nodded. "I know."

"Tell me what? Why is your hair so messed up?" Some part of my brain, the part that loved to read paranormal romance novels, tried to tell me that Axel *was* the dinosaur dragon thing. But since that was impossible, the more likely explanation was that there was a massive lizard that had been thought extinct still roaming the mountains of Colorado. When the impossible is eliminated, whatever is left is the answer, however improbable.

Axel tightened his grip around me. I looked up at him as he sighed. "Charlotte, please remember I'd never in a million years hurt you." He smiled down at me. "Neither would Asher."

"Who in the hell is Asher?" I asked.

I am Asher.

The voice in my mind sounded nothing like my own inner voice. I shook my head and looked around Axel at Ava. I was losing my damn mind, hearing voices in my head. Did they hear it, too?

"Asher is me, part of me. I am a dragon."

Chapter 19 - Axel

She didn't faint, so that was a good sign. When I said the word dragon, she pulled out of my arms, though, and sat down.

"I'm sorry. That's impossible."

Her eyes had a far-away look to them. That didn't feel like a good sign to me. "I know it's ludicrous." What should I have said? No words sounded anything but crazy.

"He's telling the truth, Char." Ava sat beside her and touched her arm.

Charlotte jerked it away. "Prove it."

She needed to see me shift. That was fine. Asher loved showing off how handsome he was. "Okay. Come out back."

"I'll wait here," Ava said delicately. She probably had no desire to see me naked, not that I wanted her to anyway.

"We'll be back in a minute." I opened the door for Charlotte. She walked past me onto the back porch but quickly stepped to the side. I got the impression she didn't want me to touch her.

Quickly, I stripped to my underwear, then walked into the middle of the backyard. "Remember, neither of us will hurt you. Not in any way." At the last second, I stepped out of the boxers and then let Asher shift.

When it finished, Asher roared, but not too loud. He wanted to show off, but not scare her. She pressed herself against the house.

Shift back. The stubborn dragon wouldn't want to go back, but she was freaked out.

He chuffed and turned in a circle, preening.

She's scared. Talk to her.

Asher looked directly at Charlotte.

Hello, mate.

The sound of her quick breaths reverberated in our ears. She wasn't terrified, like we'd thought. She was definitely scared, but I thought I sensed a bit of wonder there, as well. "Is that you in my head?" She cocked her head and squinted her eyes.

Asher moved his head in a nodding motion. *When your mind is unguarded and open, you can hear me even when we are in Axel's body.*

"I need answers," she whispered. "This is too much."

Would you like Axel's body back now?

She nodded. "No disrespect." She laughed, but it wasn't a humorous sound. It was panicked. "You are a handsome dragon."

She only said it because she was terrified of Asher, but dragons loved compliments. He let me shift back then, feeling handsome and loved.

The brat.

I yanked my underwear on, then my uniform pants. Charlotte darted into the kitchen. I finished dressing inside, then sat across from her at the table and took in her wide eyes. "That was Asher."

She nodded and made a soft sound. Kind of a squeak. "How? When? Why?" She was too overwhelmed to make much sense. She couldn't stay still. Her leg jiggled, and she rapped her fingers on the tabletop.

Ava interjected. "It's not just Axel… Maverick, James, Jury. Even Maddox is."

"They're d-d-dragons?" She raised her eyes to her friend, but she looked hurt more than curious. "I feel like a fool."

"Please," I begged. "Please don't. We are forbidden from telling until we're sure we want to spend our lives with someone. What if I told you too soon, and you flipped out and tried to expose us?"

She nodded her head. "I understand that. It makes sense. But I still feel like an utter fool."

"Maverick is our alpha. I told you we had to move away because of his hormones, which was mostly true. When an alpha comes of age and has his first shift, he gets volatile, violent. We had to go to my grandfather, because he's an alpha, too."

She looked directly at me, but I didn't like the hurt in her eyes. "You're not an alpha?"

I tried to pretend the question didn't sting. "No. Maverick is the only one in our immediate family."

She wasn't reacting. She should've been screaming or crying or slapping me. "You should know, I planned to tell you very soon. You're important to me, and I wanted you to know."

Her breathing, like a drumbeat in my ears, picked up. "I'm important to you?"

I nodded.

"Tell her the rest," Ava muttered.

Charlotte's gaze flashed between us. "What?"

"Charlotte, you're my fated mate." Might as well get it all out there without beating around the bush. "My dragon recognized you as being the perfect mate for him. He says it's more complicated than that, but for us, that's what matters."

"Fated." Her eyebrows lowered. "You're only interested in me because some magical fate guiding your inner dragon says you have to be?"

"No," I nearly shouted. "No. It made me notice you, sure. As soon as I saw and smelled you, I know we were meant to be together, but Charlotte, that didn't make me love you. I got to know you and the more I knew, the more I loved. I'm crazy about you and that has nothing to do with being fated."

Tears filled her eyes as she nodded. She didn't believe me. Damn it! I should've told her earlier, on my own terms, so that she didn't have such a shock. "I just can't help but wonder if you would've even looked at me twice if it weren't for *fate*. Of course not. I don't attract guys like you. Not without the cosmos stepping in."

"I don't know. I probably would have, because you're fucking gorgeous." She stared at me wide-eyed. "Most likely, I think yes, I would've noticed you. But I can't say for sure, because the bond slapped me in the face first thing. After that, all my emotions, all my attempts to get to know you were only because I think you're the most amazing woman in the world."

She looked away and wrapped her arms around herself.

"I would've fallen in love with you either way," I whispered.

She looked at me again, tears streaming down her face. I wanted to gather her into my arms and kiss each one away, but I didn't know how she'd react.

"Do you mean that?" she asked in the tiniest, most vulnerable voice I'd ever heard out of her mouth.

I nodded until my hair fell into my eyes. "More than I've ever meant anything in my life. You're it for me. Fated or not, I don't want anyone else ever again. I only want you, for the rest of my life." Emotion poured out of me. My throat was thick with it.

She sighed. "This is a lot to process. A lot. And I can't help but feel betrayed." She shot Ava a look when she said that. "I understand the secrecy, but it's just a lot."

Standing, she held up her hand when I tried to stand, too. "I need some space. I need to think."

Something was off with her. She was hurt and confused, but there was another emotion there I couldn't discern.

"I'm sorry," Ava said. "I wanted to tell you. Then when you started getting really into Axel, I knew it had to come from him."

Charlotte nodded. "I understand. I just have to process." She smiled, but it didn't reach her eyes like it usually did. She backed away from the table and out into the hall. "I'll see you guys later."

I started to go after her, but Ava put her hand on my arm. "Take my SUV," she called.

The jangle of the keys off the table by the front door was the only response.

"She took it," Ava said. "She'll be okay."

"I fucked this all up."

Ava patted my back. "Big brother, you really did."

I looked at her in surprise. It was the first time she'd referred to me as a brother.

I liked it.

"Thanks, little sister." I reached out and pulled her into a sideways hug. "Help me fix this?"

She laughed and squeezed me. "Of course. What are sisters for?"

What, indeed?

Chapter 20 - Charlotte

Processing everything I learned didn't happen that day. I ended up driving the SUV straight to the manor, then locking myself in my room.

Thank goodness the door had a decent lock.

Not that a dragon couldn't have gotten it open, but still.

A dragon.

My first instinct had been to run, but I wanted to make sure I didn't react out of shock. I was off the next day, too, and spent it in my room. I ventured downstairs after I saw Axel leave for work and Carla was in the kitchen.

"Oh, honey. I'm so sorry you had to find out that way." She held out her arms, but I couldn't.

"Please," I said. "I don't want to hug. Nothing personal, you've been so kind. But I feel like my world has been rocked."

She nodded. "I get it. When James showed me..." She broke off and laughed. "I didn't take it well. I was terrified of him."

Nodding, I went to the fridge to look for something to eat.

I no longer felt comfortable in the manor. A couple of days before, I would've made myself something to eat with ease, at home in the kitchen. Carla had made me feel so welcome. But knowing the big secret she'd kept—they'd all kept it—now I felt like a stranger in a strange land.

Carla tried to initiate a conversation a few times, but all I could manage were polite replies. After a few minutes, she gave up. "I'll leave you alone, dear. I'm so sorry."

She put a hand on my back for a moment, but I couldn't help it. I flinched.

My emotions warred. She'd been so kind. Hadn't I said how much I cared for her? Why couldn't I accept her apology? Because she'd gone weeks, welcoming me in her home. Treating me like a damn daughter, and didn't have the good courtesy to even give me a hint.

I'd been thinking about moving in with Axel, for the love of God!

And once again, I'd made all the wrong decisions. Next time a hot man showed interest in me, I was running for the hills.

That afternoon, I snuck downstairs again to get some food for lunch and dinner. I could've gone out, I guessed, but hiding in my room seemed preferable to risking running into anyone in town.

Who else was a dragon? Harley? Carlos? I had no way of knowing. I'd have to go back to work the next day, which would be great. I could focus on that and try to find a way to make peace with this.

And if I couldn't make peace, I'd move on. What else could I do?

James was in the kitchen this time, pouring a glass of milk. "Hello, dear."

I risked looking him in the eye, but he didn't look at me. When he'd had his glass of milk, he smiled, still not meeting my eyes, and left the room.

He couldn't even be in the room with me. He knew that I knew. Obviously, he wasn't happy about it.

Damn it. I wasn't sure I could get past this.

Axel came home from work and tapped on my door. "Come in." I hadn't locked it this time. I knew we'd have to talk.

"How was work?" I sat in the middle of my bed with my laptop in front of me. I'd been searching for real stories of shifters all day, but everything that came up was fiction.

"Long. I couldn't wait to get back here to you." He sat on the edge of the bed and held out his hand. "Would you like to go get dinner?"

I nodded, only to get more answers from him. "Nowhere far, please."

He nodded and walked us to his truck with his hand in mine. I used the drive to collect my thoughts and figure out exactly what I wanted to ask him. When we pulled in at the grocery store. I walked in with him, and he went to the deli counter and ordered two subs. After grabbing a couple of sodas and a bag of chips, he checked out and we went back to his truck.

He parked us at another overlook. The breathtaking view didn't do the same thing for me today that it had a few days ago. I wondered how many supernatural creatures roamed the earth under just the part I could see.

"Is it just your family?"

He shook his head. Once he swallowed his bite, he spoke. "There are many different types of shifters in the world. As far as I know, vampires and witches are a myth. All I've ever experienced are shifters."

My heart froze. "What other kinds?"

"There is a pack of wolf shifters here in Black Claw. They help protect our land in exchange for the right to roam it and hunt. We take care of each other that way."

I considered the concept of wolf shifters. "Any more dragons?"

"Just my family and Stefan."

Stefan. Oh, geez. Harley. "What happens if I tell?"

He put a chip in his mouth and studied my face. "Do you think anyone would believe you?"

Damn, that was a good point.

We ate in silence while I considered the fated mate thing. "Does everyone have a fated mate?"

"No. It's rare and seems to be getting rarer by the year. Though, Ava and Maverick were fated. Maybe it's something in the water up here." He chuckled, but I didn't.

I wasn't convinced he'd care about me if not for whatever it was in him that made him think he was supposed to be with me.

"What if I'd been horrible?" I asked. "What if I had a terrible personality, and I was mean-spirited?"

He stared at me, without an answer. "But you're not."

"That's my point! Maybe I am. You don't know. You could only love me because of some magical rule that says you have to."

I shook my head. I wasn't buying this fated shit. How was a person supposed to know their true feelings? It wasn't right. "Take me home, please."

He sighed and nodded. As he drove, I snuck a glance. His jaw was set and hard. Pissed.

I couldn't help it. I couldn't stop feeling doubts and fears.

My parents always said there was something wrong with me. They'd told me countless times that nobody would want me unless I changed. Got more serious about my future. Acted more responsible.

Maybe they were right after all. I'd spent my entire adult life running from that judgment and each time I tried a relationship, it ended in flames. Maybe because they were right about me all along. Something about me was fundamentally unlovable.

A dark cloud settled over me. I didn't say anything else to Axel as we pulled up in front of the house. Later that evening, locked in my room, I texted Jury and arranged for him to take me to and from work. At least I'd still feel safe from Logan that way.

I sent Axel a message to let him know he didn't need to worry about taking me, then shut the phone off. I didn't want to read his reply.

He was at work when I left the next morning, and I managed to avoid him for the next three days. I went to work, had Jury stop for some fast food or grabbed something from the cafeteria, then locked myself in my room. I still didn't want to dip into my savings if I could avoid it, and my first paycheck was due today.

Sure enough, my supervisor handed it to me. "You can cash it at the credit union downstairs." I'd never worked in a hospital big enough to have its own bank inside. "Or deposit in your account."

I didn't have an account anywhere nearby. I hadn't seen the national bank I had my savings at around Black Claw, so I stopped in the credit union on my lunch and cashed the check.

If I needed to run, now I could. It was enough money to keep me on the road for a couple of weeks, if I slept a lot of nights in my car.

I'd have to head to a warm climate.

I still wasn't sure I wanted to leave Black Claw. I loved my job. But I considered moving to the next town over. It was closer to the hospital, anyway. Then, I'd still be close to Ava. And Harley.

Jury drove me back to the manor as I mulled over my options. I could get a hotel room while I searched for an apartment. I'd have another good paycheck in two weeks. Better than this one, even.

When I walked into my bedroom, Axel was sitting on my bed. I froze in the doorway.

"Hey, can we talk?" he asked.

I nodded. Like I had a choice. "Sure."

"Why are you avoiding us?" he asked pointedly.

I set my purse down on the dresser and crossed my arms. "Why wouldn't I avoid you? This whole thing is insane!"

"We made a mistake. *I* made a mistake keeping it from you for so long." He threw up his hands and stood. "But you've had a week to come to terms with it. Surely by now you're making some peace with it."

As he walked around the bed, I moved as well. I didn't want him in my bubble, convincing me with his gorgeous eyes. "What am I supposed to say? I'm hurt. I feel betrayed. I can't just get over it like you dropped my favorite plate and broke it. You lied to me for weeks all the while romancing me!" How could I be sure he ever planned to tell me?

"I'm so sorry I hurt you." True pain crossed his face. But he was a good liar. Maybe he was a good actor, too. I'd been burned by men who seemed sincere before. "But it wasn't done maliciously. We didn't do it from a place of trying to deceive you, like some villains in a TV show. We just have to keep the secret until we're sure. I've been sure, but I didn't know how to tell you."

I nodded. "Part of me totally understands that. But, Axel, I've been hurt so badly before, by men who didn't turn into monsters."

He drew back. "Asher isn't a monster. He's intelligent and proud."

"I'm sure he is. But I think you've convinced yourself you love me to fulfill some fated mate obligation you have. It's rare, so you think you have to give in to it."

His face darkened more. "Will I ever be able to win? Will you ever let me prove to you that I've fallen head over heels in love with you?"

I didn't answer. The only thing I knew to do was to give it time, but he was pressuring me to make a decision and make my heart do what he wanted it to do.

"I'm doing the best I can, but it's like you don't want to meet me halfway. I shouldn't have to fight alone for our relationship. Are you willing to fight, too?"

I was, but that decision teetered. "I need time."

He sighed. "It's been five days. I'm not like your ex-boyfriends. I'm not a player or a user. My emotions are my own, fates be damned. You're letting your old hurts ruin something beautiful." He stopped pacing and held out his arms. "I won't fight for this relationship alone. I'll fight to hell and back with you, but not alone."

My heart finished splintering. This hurt a thousand times more than when Logan beat the shit out of me. This was my heart breaking, not my skull. "Then stop fighting," I whispered.

He stepped backward, stunned. Then he blinked several times, before turning and walking out of the room, closing the door behind him with a soft click.

I went to the closet and pulled out my biggest suitcase. I packed everything I'd need for a couple of nights. Ava could help me come back and get the rest.

Once I made sure I had work clothes, toiletries, and a couple of books to keep me company, I carried the suitcase downstairs. I'd parked around the back, so I had to go through the kitchen to get out of the house.

Axel was alone, sitting at the table.

He raised his eyes and looked at me. He'd been crying.

I rolled the suitcase around the table and toward the back door, but he didn't say a word.

I'd thought my heart was completely broken, but it shattered more when he didn't stop me.

If I wanted him to stop me so badly, why did I tell him to stop fighting for us?

Because it would never have worked. I was too broken. Too screwed up. Add dragons to my story and it was nothing more than a tale for the loony bin.

After a split-second pause at the door to give him time to stop me, I slammed it behind me and ran to my car, then threw the suitcase in my back seat.

Axel opened the back door before I got in the driver's seat. My heart soared. He'd decided to try again. To give me time. "Logan is still out there. Don't be surprised if you see someone trailing you when you're not at work." He shut the back door and pulled the shade.

Effectively locking me out. For good.

I sobbed and drove toward the hospital. There was a hotel beside it that had good reviews online.

Every few minutes I had to dash tears from my eyes as I drove, but I made it safely to the hotel. Checking in was no problem, and soon I was face down, clutching a pristine white pillow, sobbing my heartache out.

I must've fallen asleep, because the next thing I knew, someone pounded on my door.

Axel. Oh, thank goodness. I'd made a horrible mistake. I needed time, but I could've had time while being near him and not rejecting him. He'd been wonderful to me, as had his family.

I hadn't reacted well to learning shifters roamed the planet and that he noticed me because of some stupid fate.

But I didn't want to stop fighting.

"Axel," I cried as I opened the door.

Except it wasn't Axel.

It was Logan.

"Who the fuck is Axel?" he snarled and shoved his way into the room.

As I stumbled away from him, I remembered the huge knife.

It was still in the bedside drawer.

At the manor.

Chapter 21 - Axel

I'd walked out the back door when I heard her car going down the driveway out front, but not in time to stop her. I should've been faster, backed off sooner. It wasn't until the sound of the engine faded to nothing that the anger faded and regret kicked in.

Damn it. I'd messed everything up. She'd just asked for a little more time to come to terms with the fact that her entire world, the fabric of reality she understood, had been irreversibly altered.

I could've given her a few more days for that.

My heart pounded painfully. I sat on the back porch, staring out at the snow until the cold seeped to my bones. It must've been a couple of hours because it took a long time for a dragon to get cold deep inside. The fire that lived in Asher lived in me, coiled in my gut, able to spread and warm.

It stayed banked. Asher was forlorn and worried.

We should've claimed her.

That would've been worse, whatever he believed. If we'd claimed Charlotte, bitten her without warning or consent, she would've disappeared without a trace. At least this way, all of her belongings were still here. She had to come back at some point. And when she did, we would do whatever we had to do to make it right.

Ignoring the cold, I sat still on the back porch, even after I decided to do whatever I had to do to make things up to her. I argued with myself back and forth about whether or not to try calling her cell phone.

The best course of action was to give her time as she asked for. But I needed her to know that I wasn't done fighting for us. I forced myself to wait, not try to contact her yet, let her calm down. She was probably down at Ava and Maverick's right now anyway. Safe.

Snow began to fall, drifting gently down and settling on my shoulders. After a few minutes, it stopped melting. "What are you doing out here?" Maverick's voice cut through the peace of the night. I hadn't even heard him open the door.

"Charlotte left."

"When?" Maverick grabbed me under one of my arms and hauled me to my feet. "You're freezing. Come on inside." He all but carried me into the kitchen and pushed me into a chair. "What happened?"

"I told her it had been enough time for her to come to terms with what she learned about us." I hung my head. What a fool I was.

"Are you an idiot?" He threw a hand towel at my head. "Dry your hair."

"Of course I'm an idiot." I stared at Maverick as I put two and two together. "She's at your place, right?"

He shook his head. "No, I've been calling your phone, and when I couldn't get you, I came straight up here."

Worry washed over me. At least before, I'd been hurting for making such a mess of things, but I'd been sure she was safe. "I told Stefan to stay on her tail. Where's my phone?"

After I'd texted him, I'd set it on the counter. It was still there. I grabbed it and checked my missed calls and messages as I toweled my hair.

Four missed calls and three texts from Maverick. "You're a worrywart. What if I'd just been asleep?"

"I saw Charlotte's car go by. Alone. I wanted to check. After a couple of hours, I figured it had been long enough."

Stefan had sent three messages.

Found her. Following her now.

She's at a hotel. The one by the hospital.

I smelled my way to her room, but so many people being around here made it hard. She's in 312 and from the sound through the door, she's asleep. I'm waiting in the car. Parked beside hers.

"She's safe." I relayed the messages to Maverick.

He nodded. "Good. Let her rest and calm down tonight, and you can go make it right tomorrow."

I sighed and sat at the table, clutching my phone. "Do you think I can?"

He shrugged. "Walk me through everything the two of you said."

My brother, the wise woman of the Kingstons. I chuckled but told him the whole story.

When I finished, he stared at me. "You did fuck it up, didn't you?"

"That doesn't help." He was right, but I already knew that.

"Brother, honestly. I don't think it's beyond repair. Women are resilient. And she's been through so much. You've got some apologizing to do, maybe some flowers? But it's not like you cheated on her or beat her up." He held out his hands. "She's reasonable and she knows what *true* betrayal is. This isn't that."

He was right again, but partly wrong. "Yes, but it's because of what all she's been through that I should've been more patient than I was. I owe her more than a bouquet."

We continued throwing ideas back and forth about how I could apologize to Charlotte. Now that I knew she was safe, I was able to breathe a little easier. I even changed clothes while Maverick made hot chocolate the way Mom used to.

When I came back down, I realized it was only ten, and I hadn't seen Mom or Dad all evening.

"Where are our parents?" I asked.

Maverick chuckled. "Out for dinner and a movie. That weekend they took away to give you and Charlotte some space apparently made them all romantic. Mom told Ava that Dad has been like a teenager in love."

I was happy for them, and a little grossed out. "Cute. But, ugh."

Mav burst out laughing. "My thoughts exactly."

We sipped our chocolate quietly, my heart aching for Charlotte. "Should I at least text her? Let her know I'm sorry and I'll make it up to her?"

He studied his mug. "Maybe. I don't see how it could hurt. Should we call and ask Ava?"

That was a great idea. She'd know how to help me make it right. "Yes." I picked up my phone to call her, but as soon as I did, it rang.

"It's Stefan." I hit the button. "Hello?"

"You gotta get down here. Some dude dragged her out of the hotel. She wasn't fighting or screaming, but he stuffed her into a different car. I barely saw them."

No. No! Black dots crowded my vision as the situation fully set in. Charlotte's asshole ex had her. "Why? How did this happen?" I roared. Hitting the speaker button, I put the phone on the table so Maverick could hear. Asher boiled inside me, ready to shift and hunt them down by scent. Then rip Logan apart with his teeth.

"They came out the side entrance. I was parked by her car, around the building. The only reason I noticed them was he parked far enough to the side of the building that I could just see his car."

A horn came over the speaker. "Damn," he muttered.

"What was that? Was that you?" Maverick asked.

"No, I'm behind them on the highway, but there are a couple of cars in front of us. Someone pulled out in front of someone else. Probably a good thing, it would've taken his focus off of me back here, if he even noticed me."

"What did the man look like?"

"It's dark and those hotel lights aren't the best." He grunted. "They're pulling onto a back road, actually heading back toward town. Driving a silver sedan, nondescript. Four doors, four cylinders."

Maverick got to his feet. He knew as well as I did that was the car we'd seen on the surveillance video from the gas station that Logan had used his credit card at. He must've gotten some cash somewhere because he hadn't used any of his cards again since then. There'd been no word until the day he called Charlotte.

"We're on our way," Maverick said. I followed him through the house and out the front door, where his cruiser waited. I was glad he'd driven it and not his truck.

"Stay on the line, Stefan," I said.

He didn't answer. "They're turning up Brushy Road." It led way up into the mountains to dozens and dozens of hunting cabins. Most would be empty right now, as the last hunting season of the winter had just ended. The cabins would have some business in the summer with hikers and nature buffs but come September, they'd fill with hunters again.

He could go to any one of them. It would take hours or days to search them all. And more manpower than we had at the moment. "Don't let them get out of your sight."

"I'll try to slow them down," Stefan said. "He has to realize by now that I'm following them."

"Stay close, but don't do anything stupid."

We pulled onto Brushy Road several minutes later. Mav had run his lights the whole way, and had been on the phone with Carlos at the station. Carlos had hung up to get more people heading our way, as well as an ambulance. Just in case.

When we turned onto the same road, he turned off the lights. "In case we need the element of surprise."

"You should let me out. I can shift and fly to them faster," I said.

Maverick shook his head. "We're not dealing with a rogue dragon. He's human. We can't let him realize we're more than that."

He was right, damn it. But while we tried to get to them, he could hurt her.

"I've got to intervene." Stefan sounded frantic over the speakerphone. "I just heard her scream. I think he hit her."

Asher roared under my skin. He'd been holding himself in check pretty well until then, but hearing that his mate had been struck was more than he was willing to bear. Smoke poured from my nose.

"Keep it together," Maverick warned.

"Hang on!" Stefan yelled, then the phone went dead.

"Hurry up," I growled. "If you don't get to them, I'm going to shift in this car."

"Asher!" Maverick yelled and careened around a bend. The mountain curves on this road were hairpin and dangerous on a good day. Let alone in the middle of the night with fresh snow on the ground. "Listen to me! Let Axel and me handle this. Don't force the shift. I know you want to rip this man limb from limb, but he's human. You've got to let us take care of him. I promise we will."

Asher calmed slightly. I knew Maverick was avoiding using his alpha power out of respect for my position and resentment. "You'll have to do it," I said. "Asher is barely holding himself back."

Maverick slowed the car to go around a particularly sharp curve and opened his mouth again. This time his words were laced with the power of his dragon, Zephyr.

"Asher, you will not shift until the human or any other humans that come to help are out of the area. You will wait until Axel is alone."

Asher heard that. He drew back, chastised by his alpha. "He won't shift," I said. Asher was pissed. He didn't like it, not when our mate was involved. But he wouldn't break a direct order from the alpha. He couldn't. It would be painful to even contemplate it.

The headlights flashed upon a wreck. Maverick slammed on the brakes and narrowly avoided hitting one of the cars. When the lights illuminated it, I realized it was Stefan's.

He was struggling to get out of the front of his car without shifting. I smelled his shift from inside the cruiser.

Launching from the car, I ran past Stefan to find Charlotte, and realized Stefan hadn't done much damage to his car, but the adrenaline had put him too close to a shift inside the vehicle. He had to stop it or get out.

Logan staggered out of the driver's seat of the little silver car, but Charlotte's head was just visible inside. It looked like her side of the vehicle had hit the guardrail before the car spun around, resting with the front end pointed at the rail. At least that meant I could get her out.

The door handle broke off in my hand as I yanked so hard, but it was jammed shut, probably from hitting the rail.

Logan stumbled around the car, coming toward me. "Get away," he said, one hand on his head.

I wanted to rip his throat out, but I had to make sure Charlotte was okay first, so I shoved him out of the way and toward Maverick and circled the car, climbing into the driver's seat. "Charlotte. Wake up, baby. I'm here. You're safe now." Looking out the window, I saw Maverick holding that son of a bitch back. I'd deal with him in a minute.

Blood trickled from a cut on her scalp. Damn him. If I'd claimed her, she'd have been hardier. Harder to hurt.

Stefan crowded in behind me at the car door. I ignored the sounds of Maverick arguing with Logan. I didn't want my brother to handle him, I wanted to do it myself but checking on Charlotte was priority one.

"He hit her," Stefan said. "That's when I heard her scream, so I rear-ended them, but I was a little off-center. I sent both of us into a tailspin."

"You're damn lucky she didn't break through the barrier." I unbuckled her and pulled her into my arms. Maneuvering her across the console and out the driver's side was difficult, but I managed it.

She came to as I stood and looked up at me in relief as tears rolled down her cheeks. I'd never been so happy to look into her gorgeous blue eyes. "Oh, Axel." Charlotte buried her head against me and sobbed. "I'm so glad you're here." Relief and appreciation rolled off of her in waves.

"I won't ever let you out of my sight again," I promised. My heart swelled with love for my mate, and the desire to keep her safe. I couldn't believe I'd let her almost be seriously hurt by that dickhead again. "Nothing like this will ever happen to you again. I'm so sorry." I pressed my cheek to hers and whispered. "You can have all the time in the world. I'll wait for you until the end of the Earth." I meant it to the core of my being.

Asher meant it more. He wanted to shift and lift her into the air, carrying her away to hide forever.

Of course, that wasn't an option.

She squeezed my neck. "Thank you. I love you."

Those words sent a jolt of magic to my heart. The cold that hadn't left me since my time sitting on the porch washed away in a bath of warmth. Even Asher's anger hadn't warmed me inside. Charlotte's love did.

"Can you wait for me right here?" I asked. "Are you injured badly?"

She shook her head. "No. Probably another mild concussion, but nothing major."

I carefully set her in the driver's seat of Maverick's cruiser and nodded to Stefan. "Take care of her."

He nodded gravely. "With my life."

After a second of smiling reassuringly at Charlotte, I turned to face Logan. Maverick had him crowded against the guardrail. My brother hadn't engaged him, not physically, besides holding him back when needed. I was so grateful he'd waited to let me handle Logan; I could've kissed Mav. Punishing Logan for his actions was mine.

Rushing past Maverick, I reared my fist back and punched the cruel man. I couldn't put my full strength behind it—It would've killed him instantly.

I felt like I was toying with a child. Logan reared back but caught himself on the guardrail. He pushed forward and lunged at me, like a football player trying to sack the quarterback.

It was laughably easy to sidestep him.

The distant sound of sirens pricked my ears and took my attention for a split second, giving Logan a chance to sweep me off my feet.

Oh, so he knew a little bit of fighting. Good. It made it more fun to destroy him.

We danced back and forth as the sirens grew louder. I let him believe he'd gotten me a couple of times, taking a punch to the jaw and stomach.

Then, when the ambulance and Carlos were almost there, I smiled at Logan. "You'll never see her again. You'll never touch her. You'll dream at night of what you lost but mark me…" I walked closer to him. He'd stopped trying to fight and stared at me, his fists clenched at his sides. I grabbed his throat and squeezed. "If I ever see your face again, I will kill you."

Kill him. Bathe in his blood.

For once, Asher's advice seemed reasonable. I squeezed and Logan's face turned purple. He gasped, trying to speak even though my fingers were cutting off his air supply.

"You have to let go," Maverick said. "There will be a lot of people here in just a few seconds."

I tightened my grip, Asher panting for blood inside me. I could've done it. I could've ended his life, removed all possibility of the threat of him ever hurting anyone again.

"We'll make sure he goes to jail until he's a frail old man." Maverick put his hand on my flexed bicep. "But you can't kill him."

His reason broke through, and I realized he spoke the truth without forcing me with his alpha influence.

I released Logan, and he fell to the ground, his legs collapsing underneath him. Panting, he stared up at me with pure hatred in his eyes.

I squatted next to him and I smiled again, but I knew it was a sadistic, twisted expression. "You're alive because I don't want to deal with paperwork."

With that, I left him and went to Charlotte, gathering her in my arms and turning to the ambulance, which had just parked.

I let her explain it all to the paramedics, who I didn't know well. They were new recruits. I had no doubt we'd get to know each other in time, but for now, I only had eyes for Charlotte.

They loaded her in the back, giving us a great view of Carlos not so gently cuffing Logan and stuffing him in the back of his car. We followed the car down the mountain, and when we reached the highway, they went right, toward the police station. We went left, to the hospital and toward help for my Charlotte.

Chapter 22 - Charlotte

From the time they released me, with a warning about concussions and taking it easy, Axel carried me. My car was still at the hotel next door and he walked there with me tucked in his arms. "I can walk," I whispered.

He laughed. "I know. But I can't put you down. My arms won't unbend."

I sighed and buried my face in his neck. I was sore and tired, but there was nowhere in the world I'd rather have been than right there. My keys were in my purse in the hotel room. Luckily, the sleepy receptionist remembered me and let us in the room. She almost didn't with me looking the way I did. "We went for some food and got in a car wreck," I explained.

That lit a fire under her. Her face softened. "Oh, you poor dear. Did you have the hospital check you out?"

I nodded and she clasped her hands together. "Let me make you a key."

In minutes, we were in the elevator with Axel's arms still wrapped firmly around me. He didn't act like he was winded in the slightest. I guessed it was the dragon in him. He was fit, but no man could carry me that far without at least a bit of fatigue.

It was hot. Very, very hot.

We got into the hotel room, and I remembered what a mess we'd left it. "Time to put me down," I said. "I want to fix this."

The lamp was on its side, luckily not broken. There was a small table and chair set in the corner, and one of the chairs was on its back. I'd fallen over that fighting him.

"You'll do no such thing," he said, placing me gently on the bed. "Don't move."

Axel made quick work of the room. The TV had fallen back against the wall but didn't fall to the floor. Somehow, nothing was broken, just disheveled. I got lucky.

My suitcase, which I'd left open at the end of the bed, had been knocked onto the floor and the contents fell out. He even folded my clothes and placed them neatly back inside the case but left it on the floor.

When he finished, he turned to me with a lost expression. He didn't know what to do now. We were in such an awkward place. "Come here," I whispered.

He climbed onto the bed beside me and I curled myself around him. He hummed deep in his chest. "I love you," he said. I opened my mouth to tell him I loved him, too, but he kept talking. "I love who you are. You're kind and funny. And you lick your lips after taking a long drink in a way that is cute and sexy. You want to think the best of people no matter what's going on, and you can't stand being idle. You want to work and help and do good things, otherwise, you wouldn't be a nurse. You're kind to my mom, even though she's a terrible busybody." I laughed at that. His mom was an angel.

"I love you because you're so damn lovable, Charlotte. Don't ever forget that for one second. You stole my heart. When I thought maybe I couldn't fix what I broke by pushing you, my heart broke into a million pieces. I knew as soon as I heard you drive away that I'd made a horrible mistake."

His words soothed my soul and hurt feelings, but he wasn't done.

"I can't tell you what went through my mind when you were unconscious in the car." He squeezed me closer. "You don't have to believe it. But I'm in love with you. Nothing's going to change that."

We clung to each other, both of us too upset to speak for a few moments. "I love you." I needed to say it again. I needed him to hear it. "I know it's crazy. We've known each other only weeks, and I still don't completely have Logan out of my life."

"You do now. He'll go away for a long time for attempted kidnapping. He's gone, baby. Forever." He paused and sighed. "Can you tell me what happened?"

I knew he'd ask soon. I dreaded recounting it, but he needed to know. "I didn't even look when he knocked." I sobbed against his chest, feeling like a total idiot. "I just assumed it was you."

Axel squeezed me close. "I wish it had been. I was telling myself to give you space, let you have time."

Well, that *was* what I'd asked for. "I don't want space anymore. I don't need time."

"Good, because I'm never letting you go. You'll have to go to work with me. We'll figure out a way to use the bathroom while still touching. Our love will get us through it." My tears dissolved into laughter as he continued to describe how we'd manage to stay together. "What happened after he got in?"

I gestured around the room. "We fought. He didn't hit me too hard but threatened to. I had to stop. I was terrified he'd give me another concussion or do worse this time than last, especially since he'd had time to stew on it and get more upset."

"That's understandable."

"After that, he just ranted at me until he figured out Stefan was behind us. I saw him pull out. I knew he was there." I shifted in his arms, getting as close to him as I could. "I knew you'd come."

"Did he say how he found you and why he waited so long to come?" Axel asked.

That was one of the few questions I'd asked him. What made him wait? "Yes. He had hacked into my cell phone account and had it set to email him if the GPS pinged. He got one ping off of it the whole time after I left.

I think it was the time Ava turned it on to get my contacts out of it to put on the new phone."

He grunted. "I hadn't thought of that. In my line of work, I probably should have. When you told us you turned it off, I assumed for good. How'd he get your new number to call you at the hospital?"

"Well, I had no idea he'd figured out my password." I had to get online and change all my passwords. "And the phone number was a bit of stupidity on my part," I said. "The only thing I can think of is that I'd written it down and left it on my boss's door so that she could call me if she needed me. I'd just done it that morning. He must've found it and acted immediately." Knowing he'd been that close to me without me having any idea still gave me chills.

"All I could think of was how I didn't want the last things we said to each other to be the last things we'd said." The argument we had ran through my mind over and over on the ride with Logan. "I thought he was going to kill me." My heart froze with remembered fear. "I just prayed for you to get there faster."

"What made him hit you?"

Ugh. That hadn't been my best idea. "He kept saying he was going to kill Stefan as soon as we got stopped. He told me to shut up several times, but I didn't listen. I kept telling him to pull over, that he could let me out and disappear before he got in worse trouble. I kept on and on, until he clocked me. It dazed me, and the next thing I knew, I guess Stefan rear-ended us. I don't remember anything after that until you had me in your arms."

I buried my face in his chest, gathering my thoughts. When I looked into his eyes, I saw the love he felt for me there. "I don't want you to leave me. Don't let me go. I want to be your fated mate. Your woman. Everything and anything you need. You've been by my side since the first day in the pharmacy. You've been everything I've needed you to be as I recovered and came back to myself. I want to be that for you, forever."

His mouth touched mine softly, with reverence. He moved to the corners of my lips, then my cheeks. I moaned as his lips trailed down my neck. We hadn't been this intimate since the first time.

"I have a question," I said breathlessly as his hands slid up my back.

"Yes?" He mumbled against my collarbone.

"Why did you back off? Sexually?"

He sat up and stared into my eyes. "Because I respect you. I wanted you to know I wanted you for you, not your body. Not sex."

Damn. His words were the perfect aphrodisiac. If his declarations of love hadn't done it, telling me he waited out of respect for me did. I pushed my lips to his. No more sweet. Our kisses grew more and more heated and passionate as our hands roamed one another's bodies.

"Claim me," I whispered. "I don't know exactly what that means, but I've heard you say it."

"It means I bite you. It will be a moment of pain, but then the bite increases your orgasm."

Shit, I liked a bite any day. "Do it," I demanded.

He growled, but this time it wasn't with anger. Lust, desire, and love pulsed over me. "Whoa," I whispered. Wiggling out of his arms a little, I grabbed the hem of my shirt and yanked it over my head. I'd only taken my bra off before collapsing in the hotel bed so many hours before. I still wore the scrub top and bottom from work what felt like another lifetime ago. Axel fell on my breasts like they'd save his life, massaging and lifting them until he could suck my nipple into his mouth.

I sighed as he suckled, the feeling of desire shooting up and down my body, from my nipples straight to my clit. I needed him on it or in me or something. I had to have more.

Shimmying out of my pants was a bit trickier than the shirt, but I managed it quickly. I'd put on a thong that morning. I didn't wear them often, but now I was glad I did.

Axel moaned when he saw me naked except for the black lace thong. "You're exquisite."

I laughed and stretched out beside him, running my hands up my stomach and over my breasts. "Strip, big boy."

He stood beside the bed and unbuttoned his uniform shirt. He'd taken his belt off as soon as he laid me on the bed when we arrived.

The slow reveal of his defined muscles and dusting of chest hair served to increase my desire. Every inch he exposed made me squirm, his eyes glued to my body the entire time.

When his dick came into view, I sighed. It was as nice as I remembered. Not enormous, but enough to make me clench my inner muscles, eager to feel it rubbing my inner walls, drawing a rare vaginal orgasm from me.

I sat up on the bed and scooted to the edge. Taking him in my hand, I stroked his already hard cock, tightening as I reached the base. He grunted and leaned his hips forward, pulling back as I stroked. I wasn't even sure he realized he was doing it.

When I saw him close his eyes, I leaned forward and popped the tip between my lips, sucking him in to swirl my tongue around his head.

He gasped and his fingers flew to my hair, burying in my tresses and gripping. "Charlotte," he moaned, nearly a beg.

Exploring his dick, I licked and sucked my way up one side and down the other, familiarizing myself with his body. His balls weighed heavy in my other hand as I gave them the softest of massages. When we'd had sex more often, or at least time to discuss it, I'd venture to that spot behind his sack—or farther.

I used my hand and lips to suck and stroke him, finding a rhythm to my movements and moans, until his grip on my hair tightened. Once it did, I knew I couldn't push him further or he might have his orgasm before I was ready for him to.

Leaning back, I stuck out my chest and swirled my nipples against his cock. "Shit, Charlotte," he whispered. "That's hot."

I laughed and scooted up on the bed, leaving him plenty of room to join me. "Roll over," he whispered. "I saw you come last time, this time I want to hold you while you come apart in my arms."

He helped me position on my right side, then he tucked himself around me. I figured he'd slip in behind me and make love to me that way, but he surprised me.

Axel reached around and tucked his hand between my legs. I raised my left leg to give him room. The angle meant he couldn't get far inside, but he pressed his finger to my clit and lightly moved back and forth.

I moaned, throwing my head back on his shoulder and panting slowly as his finger teased me. "Axel, please."

"Oh, do you want more?" he asked. "Like this?"

He increased the pressure, letting the nub slip out from under his finger each time he moved from one side to the other. When it slipped free, it sent a zing of intense pleasure through me.

He removed his hand for a moment, pressing against the small of my back. I arched and felt his cock head pressing against my entrance.

When I stuck my ass out, he slipped inside, filling and stretching. I was so wet; we needed no lube or help. A few small strokes and he was fully seated, filling me again like we'd been designed to love each other.

Once he was inside, he reached his hand around again and as he flexed in and out of my body, his finger built up a clitoral orgasm. He moved faster and faster, his hips making the ridges of his head catch on my G-spot to build a vaginal orgasm and his finger pressing my sensitive nub and building another orgasm there.

"I want to come with you," he whispered. "Especially since I'm claiming you. Let me know when you're close."

It didn't take long with his double assault. He moved faster and harder, sweat slicking our bodies as we slid together. "I'm almost there," I gasped. I'd been trying to hold my cries back, not sure how soundproofed the walls were. I didn't succeed much longer.

He grabbed my hip with his right hand, pressed my clit hard with his left, slammed into me as hard as he could, and then... Oh, wow. He bit.

Axel's teeth sank into my shoulder and the burst of pain was only seconds long. Behind it roared the mother of all orgasms. My body tensed up from neck to toes, a low yell erupting from my mouth.

Goosebumps danced across my body as I convulsed, my vaginal walls clenching and unclenching of their own accord, over and over. When he pulled his teeth from my shoulder, the orgasm began to wane, but vibrations continued deep inside my core for a good minute. When he pulled out of me, the liquid that trickled out could've been his or mine.

We hadn't given a condom a second thought. I didn't care one whit. I was on birth control, and Ava had told me over the phone that dragons couldn't pass human STDs. I had no worries about an infection.

My orgasm had been so intense I'd ejaculated. I'd read about female ejaculation, which was different from squirting and tried to walk ex-boyfriends through helping me achieve it. I'd tried toys and videos.

This was the first time it'd happened.

When I calmed down and relaxed, the hormones from the orgasm flooding my body, I realized there was more than that.

I felt Axel. In the back of my mind, I was aware of him. Not like I could read his mind, but I was fairly sure I'd be able to track him down anywhere in the world. And I thought maybe I felt a bit of his euphoria? This feeling wasn't just my own.

"Welcome to the Kingston clan, mate," Axel whispered. "You're mine now. And I'm yours. Forever."

I laid my head back on his shoulder again so he could press his cheek to mine. His words registered. "Wait," I said. "Forever?"

He laughed. "Not literally. We will live a few hundred years at best."

Sitting up, I shifted around until I faced him. I needed to see his face for this.

"You're serious? A few hundred years?"

He nodded.

I collapsed on the pillow, my hands on Axel's chest.

"Cool."

He chuckled and pulled me close. "Probably should've mentioned that before."

I snorted. "Probably."

Chapter 23 - Axel

"Take your tongue out of Charlotte's throat, and let's go." Maverick pulled on the back of my shirt. He, Stefan, Carlos, and I were due for guys' night out. I'd been putting it off, and Maverick had told me he'd drag me from the house if I didn't go tonight.

I'd spent more time in Charlotte than out since I claimed her two and a half months before. I mused about all the time we'd spent together as I walked to Ava's SUV. Jury and Maddox, as they were both under twenty-one, were our designated drivers tonight. We'd pick everyone up, then they'd come get us when we were done and take everyone home.

Their day would come, and we'd play their DDs then, keep them safe.

We talked about the construction of Charlotte's and my new house on the way to get the guys.

"Have you told her about it yet?" Maverick asked.

"Not yet. The frame is up. I picked the layout, but I'm going to tell her before any decorations are picked so that she can do it exactly how she'd like."

Carlos and Stefan seemed in a good mood, but the closer we got to the bar with the full SUV, the more I realized Stefan was being quiet.

I didn't push it until we all had our first beers. "Out with it," I said. Stefan looked around the room until he realized I was speaking to him.

He choked on his beer. "Me?"

"Yes, you. Why have you been so quiet?"

Maverick nodded. "Yeah, you're almost sort of sad."

Stefan sighed and drank, ignoring us. "I'm fine," he said testily.

"Come on, dude." Carlos waved over the server. "Another round on my tab," he said. When they came, he put one in front of Stefan. "What's bothering you?"

The table jostled as Stefan adjusted in his chair. "I messed up."

Now we were getting somewhere. "How'd you mess up?" I asked.

"You know that time we crashed girls' night?" he asked.

We all nodded. "Harley. I'd met her before but only suspected. The more time goes by and the more I see her, the more I'm sure that… she's my fated mate."

Oh, damn. "That's not the sort of thing you can just ignore."

He hung his head. "I know. But I'm not in a place for a mate. I know she's got a sick grandmother, and she's so good. Pure. Sweet." He moaned and dropped his head to the table. "She's perfect. I'd just ruin her and drag her down. I don't even have a real place of my own to live."

"How can you resist the pull?" Maverick asked. "That was a good three months ago."

"It's been torture. I have to stay away...from..." He trailed off and looked past me toward the door.

I smelled the new people as they walked in. And judging by the expression on Stefan's face, I knew exactly who it was.

"Hey, guys!" Harley's bright voice hit my ears, and I grimaced on Stefan's behalf. "This is Victor."

Carlos, Maverick, and I gave a grudging hello to the man who had his arm around Harley. Stefan stared at his beer.

Harley gave him a quizzical look but waved and walked to an open table toward the back of the room.

Stefan watched them once they'd passed us, with the most longing look on his face. "Stef, man, a fated mate is a blessing. That won't last. She'll feel the pull toward you, just not as strong as you feel toward her."

He looked back at his beer, then chugged it. "I need another. It's all for the best, anyway."

Uh-oh. Here we go again.

Printed in Great Britain
by Amazon

79164522R00241